# BEADBONNY ASH

For this very unusual story, the author has immersed
herself in the Celtic culture of the sixth century, with
the Western Isles for its principal setting. A party of
modern teenage girls and boys find themselves magi-
cally transported into this distant world and *Beadbonny Ash* tells how their twin existences are resolved.
Winifred Finlay's ability to create atmosphere has
never been bettered, as she takes us and her characters
back to the times of the Picts, the Kingdom of Dalriada
and the coming of St Columba to Argyll. *Beadbonny Ash* will entrance and delight all Winifred
Finlay's fans and her vivid creation of another age will
surely attract new young readers.

*By the same author*

THE CASTLE AND THE CAVE   ·

ALISON IN PROVENCE

MYSTERY IN THE MIDDLE MARCHES

ADVENTURE IN PRAGUE

DANGER AT BLACK DYKE

SUMMER OF THE GOLDEN STAG

THE CRY OF THE PEACOCK

SINGING STONES

In 1970 *Danger at Black Dyke* received from the Mystery Writers of America the Edgar Allan Poe Award for the best juvenile mystery story of the year. It was the first time the Award had been made to a non-American.

# Contents

Degged with dew, dappled with dew
Are the groins of the braes that the brook treads through,
Wiry heathpacks, flitches of fern,
And the beadbonny ash that sits over the burn.

*Gerard Manley Hopkins*

# 1 "Blood Red and Dancing . . ."

IT TOOK all four of them so completely by surprise—the jarring crash of thunder—that no one moved until the last angry mutterings had died away.

"Some prototype breaking the sound barrier," Kenneth said, recovering first and picking himself slowly off the rock face where Bridie had just sent him sprawling. Shock rapidly gave way to anger: if she hadn't been a girl he'd have returned the shove with interest, to see how she liked having the knees of her jeans torn and her elbows scraped. But of course it wasn't the unexpectedness of the noise overhead or the damage to himself or his clothes which really annoyed him. It was Bridie's treachery.

Ever since she'd come to stay with them in Oban, he'd done more than anyone else for her. At first it was just to please his parents, and to keep her out of Sheena's hair while she was sitting her exams, but before long he found that he quite liked her. He'd thought that she liked him in return. She'd coaxed him into confiding in her, and now she'd just wrecked his latest and most cherished game. Deliberately.

"It didn't sound like a plane to me," Bridie said, shaking off her fear as she placed her shoe more firmly inside the footprint cut in the rock. She smiled with malicious satisfaction as she saw Kenneth wince. Why should she play his silly games and crown him king just because there'd once been a king here in Argyll with the same name as his? In this age of women's rights she thought it very fitting that she'd beaten him to it and appointed herself queen.

"You can be my devoted page," she said, in a condescending tone.

"They didn't have pages in those times," Kenneth muttered furiously, and scooping water from the hollowed-out basin nearby, he flung it at Bridie.

"Oh, dear!" Sheena looked in dismay at the black, jagged tear across her notebook, made when her pencil slipped and the point broke. A whole afternoon wasted, she thought, staring now through the protective glass at the boar engraved on the rock beside her. She'd got it exactly right—the prowling movement, the all-seeing round eye, the sensitive, tapir-like snout—and then the thunder had nearly frightened her out of her wits. "I'll have to do it again," she mourned, "and it'll never come right a second time. Never."

"What on earth's got into John?" Kenneth demanded, watching with interest as his elder brother came racing up the steep hillside towards them. "Think you're on the rugger field again?" he shouted. "Or did a horse-fly get you?"

John MacDonald ignored his brother and brushed aside his sister's detaining hand as she sought to show him the damage to her holiday project. Three years of medical training were forgotten, natural patience and tolerance were lost somehow when that terrific crash had roused him from idle relaxation among the bracken and heather, and it had seemed as if someone had called to him from the top of the hill here, called desperately and urgently for help.

"You little idiot!" he shouted, seizing Bridie and shaking her, so that her shoe no longer nestled within the outline of the footprint. "What do you think you're doing?"

Taken aback, she stared up at him, making no attempt to break free. "I . . . we . . . we were just playing," she stammered. John, the doctor —well, almost a doctor—who already knew so much about curing people who were ill, who understood what went on in people's minds without their having to put it into words, who knew the terrible tragedy of her life—how could he stare at her like this? Quickly she looked round at Kenneth.

"Weren't we? Only playing, I mean. They had queens as well as kings in those days. You told me so yourself. Queens like Boudicca. I'd have crowned you afterwards. You know I would."

Kenneth sighed as his anger evaporated. Bridie was on the verge of tears, and whether they were genuine or not, he hated to see her cry.

"Of course you would. She beat me to it, John, that's all. No need to look so mad. You must have been dreaming or something."

"Me? Dreaming? I wasn't even asleep."

"O.K.," Kenneth agreed, in much too reasonable a tone. "You weren't asleep. That noise that sounded exactly like snoring to us was just you breathing in the pure air of Argyll after months of Edinburgh pollution."

Perhaps he had been dreaming, John thought uncomfortably. Certainly he was tired to the very marrow of his bones. He was, he knew, a slightly below average student academically, which meant he had to work harder than most; but he was a better than average sportsman, which meant—well, one way and another it added up to the fact that he'd been burning the candle at both ends. He'd take himself in hand when they went to Mull. Out of doors all day, fishing, walking and climbing: studying all evening and eight hours sleep every night. Dreaming that someone needed the help of a third-year undergraduate was a classic case of conceit and one which made him feel most uncomfortable. Matters weren't improved by the hurt way Bridie continued to regard him. At the back of his mind was this queer idea that somehow she'd come between him and that cry for help. What nonsense.

"Sorry, infant." He patted her on the head. "Kenneth's right. I must have been dozing. Hope I didn't scare you."

"As a matter of fact . . . " Bridie began stiffly, but John had turned away from her and was now trying to think what could be done to salvage his sister's damaged sketch.

With difficulty Bridie controlled genuine tears. For the first time since she'd come to Scotland she felt unwanted and misunderstood.

Perhaps misunderstood was the wrong word, at any rate as far as Kenneth was concerned. He understood her all right. She couldn't think now what had made her behave so selfishly. Digging into the back pocket of her jeans, she produced a limp bar of milk chocolate and broke it into two.

"Here," she said, thrusting the larger piece at Kenneth. Somehow she couldn't bring herself to apologize. "We'll come back another time and do it properly." She lowered her voice to signify that once again the matter was a secret between the two of them. "We'll dress up the way they did in those days and have a proper crown, and I'll write words for us both to say. You'll have the longest speeches of course, promising to be as brave and cunning as that boar down there."

"O.K." Kenneth was more prone to lose his temper than John or Sheena, but he was too good-natured to remain angry with anyone for long.

"What about clearing off and planning it now?" Bridie suggested, leading the way up towards the top of the hill until they were out of sight and hearing of the other two. "You'll probably have to look things up, won't you? You must have the right kind of dagger. And sword. Anything else?"

"A chariot would be super, but. . . ."

"Why not?" Bridie asked recklessly. To establish the old relationship she'd have promised him the moon if he'd asked for it. "With knives attached to the wheels. We could borrow a couple of horses from the farm down there and you could come charging along the old causeway and up through the hollow where the fortress gates used to be."

Overhead a planing seagull whirled and looped, while lightning flickered across the sky, turning the Sound of Jura momentarily from blue to silver.

"That's the old well," Kenneth said, darting off suddenly in the direction of a broken iron grid which covered a black hole in the turf-covered rock. Kneeling down, he peered into the darkness. "Anyone there?" he shouted.

"There . . . there . . . there," the shaft echoed eerily, as though the words were spinning down into the very heart of the hill.

Necks outstretched, five swans flew across the Great Moss towards the forests of Kilmichael, the heavy creak of their wings reminding him of the sound of Calum's oars when he took them fishing on Loch Scridain.

"Listen! Where's that music coming from?" Bridie cried suddenly.

"What music?" For a moment Kenneth paused in his search for a stone to throw down into the well: he wanted to find out how deep it was and whether or not there was water at the bottom. "I can't hear anything."

"The harp music and the singing. You must be able to hear them, Kenneth. You must."

Such music as she had never heard before—fingers plucking at strings to draw out a tune which made her blood run slower and slower with longing; a woman singing harshly, compellingly, a strange air in a strange tongue, so that her whole being seemed about to dissolve in an agony of love.

Slowly, almost against her will, she left Kenneth, walked up to the crest of the hillock, and there, in the hollow, she saw them.

The singer and the harp player were one—an old woman seated on a boulder. Grey, dishevelled hair hid her face and a shapeless grey robe drooped round her body; knotted veins disfigured the back of the one hand she could see. Two men, their backs towards her, looked down on a low couch where lay a still figure covered by a coarse woollen blanket. One of the men was tall and lean and taut: he wore a peculiar head-dress of coloured feathers and a long cloak of animal skins. In cruel contrast, his companion was stunted and deformed, with reddish-brown hair falling on to a greasy black tunic.

Suddenly the singer changed from her own language to English . . .

We call from the star-heart of Dunadd
We call the Healer from the Unborn Years.
His cures are mightier than our cures,
His spells are stronger than our spells.
His magic is greater than our magic because he has travelled far on
    the Wings of Time.
Once he belonged to us—
Now he must return to us.

The Hill of Dunadd is calling
And the Moine Mhor.
The Great White One is calling from the Especially Sacred Forest.
For the sake of the prince who is sorely wounded we call to you, O
    Healer from the Unborn Years.
Come back to us.
Come.
Come.

"What on earth are you staring at, Bridie?" Kenneth demanded as he joined her on the hill top. "There's nothing here. Come on back and help me count how long it takes for a stone to reach the bottom of the well." Impatiently he seized her arm and immediately stiffened. Now he too could see the figures, hear the music calling to them so insistently.

At first he was dominated by curiosity: he wanted to hurry down to the strange group, ask them who they were and what they were doing there, but at the same moment that Bridie took a step forward, he was suddenly aware they were both beset by danger of some kind. The quivering, pulsating music which had attracted him at first now seemed to press against his ear drums as though it were trying to annihilate his mind and his body too.

"Don't listen!" he cried fiercely, pulling Bridie round so that she could no longer see the group, and the glazed look slowly left her eyes. "Let's get away from here—now."

Frightened of they knew not what, they fled back the way they had come. A hare scuttled from a nearby rock, stared at them for a shocked moment and then zigzagged to the safety of a clump of bracken, while the drone of a foraging bee changed to anger as they charged carelessly through his patch of wild thyme and lady's bedstraw.

Once they were out of sight of the old well they slowed down and came to a halt, subdued and perplexed.

"Someone ought to mend that cover," Kenneth remarked. He'd meant to say something else, but he couldn't remember what it was now. He'd a vague idea something had happened in the hollow, but it must just have been his imagination, he decided, because he couldn't remember seeing anyone there at all.

"Yes," Bridie agreed, giving Kenneth a covert glance. She could remember nothing of what they'd seen or talked about since they left the other two. She didn't even know what cover he was referring to.

Preoccupied, they drifted back to the engraved rock where John and Sheena still stood, contemplating the torn sketch.

It was obvious they'd never been missed, Bridie thought, searching in her pocket for the last bar of chocolate and giving Kenneth considerably less than half. Perhaps they'd never left the rock. Perhaps they'd been here all the time. She glanced at Kenneth again, but he was whittling away at a piece of wood he had found on the beach that morning, his face serene and unconcerned.

For a moment terror gripped her. For over a year now she had moved in and out of an imaginary world, peopled with men and women of her own creation, the memory of her adventures always remaining with her. Now it seemed as though she had entered her secret world without choosing to do so herself, and, what was worse, she had left it without any recollection of what had happened there.

She stared around as though searching for a clue to what had happened. What a marvellous stage this great carved rock would make, with the engraved boar, the hollowed-out pool still half-full of water, and the outline of a king's foot. That was what the MacDonalds had brought her to see, not because she was interested in the old Picts and Celts, but because they were.

"Bridie!"

She jumped at the sharpness of John's tone.

"You really ought to cut out eating chocolate all the time. It's bad for your teeth and it worries Mother when you don't eat your meals. If you're not careful you'll end up fat and spotty, and you won't like that, will you?"

Because she knew how plain she was, how overweight she had been when she first arrived at Easter, Bridie flushed.

"Just because you're going to be a doctor—" she began angrily, and then quickly changed both argument and tone. "You ought to be kinder to me than anyone because you'll soon be a doctor."

The kid was right, John thought, immediately remorseful. What had come over him to keep on at her like that? She hadn't meant to interfere . . . to prevent him from. . . . He rubbed his chin with the knuckles of his left hand. What on earth was he thinking about?

"Don't forget that Bridie really has lost weight since she came here, and the doctor did say that the occasional bar of chocolate wouldn't do her any harm," Sheena said, trying to smooth matters over.

"Bridie's idea of occasional and her doctor's are two different things," Kenneth said, determined to aggravate matters. He was sure there was something he'd wanted to tell his brother and sister, and now it had gone. It was all Bridie's fault—Bridie who had spoiled the game he had so looked forward to. "Dr Johnnie's right," he added, staring at Bridie. "You've got a spot coming already, right on the tip of your nose."

"It's time we thought of going home," Sheena declared, aware that the happy atmosphere of the afternoon had gone and that the longer they stayed there, the more things would deteriorate. "The boys can bring the rugs and picnic basket down. Come on. We'll go and have a look at the river." Seizing Bridie by the hand, she led the way down the steep, winding path, talking cheerfully of her new school project on this ruined fort of Dunadd, which had once been the centre of the Celtic kingdom of Dalriada.

Bridie nodded her head and gave an occasional smile. If Sheena hadn't been such a nice girl—and there were times when she hated that very niceness, and then despised herself for hating it—she'd have told Sheena that she wasn't interested in history in general, in Scottish history in particular, and that a few months previously, couldn't have told anyone where Argyll was.

O.K. So those Celts were the ancestors of the MacDonalds, and Kenneth wanted to play at Picts and Celts instead of Cowboys and Indians, and Sheena had chosen to do a project on them. Fair enough. Just so long as they didn't expect her to get all worked up about them.

At the back of her mind she knew she was being less than fair to the MacDonalds. They never expected anything from her. They'd accepted her as one of the family and then given in to her and spoiled her. And she'd taken advantage of their kindness and made no attempt to hide her unhappiness. If she was honest with herself, she'd admit things had changed for her and she really was happier—no, "happy" was not a word she could ever apply to herself again—all right then, she was less unhappy than she had been in England. But something had gone wrong this afternoon and for the first time they had quarrelled with her. It was something to do with this ruined fort, and the sooner she got away from it the better.

She returned to what Sheena was saying just long enough to trace the dark blue of the Add as it made its leisurely way through the flat fields of the Moine Mhor—the Great Moss—almost encircling the hill of Dunadd before flowing into Loch Crinan and then out into the stormy waters of the Atlantic.

The river and sea reminded her of boats, and she tried to recall some of the ships which tied up at the harbours of Oban, their names so affectionately listed by Kenneth, along with their performances, weight, crews and a host of technical details quite lost on her. Dinghies, ketches, yawls and sloops she could remember, even though she could not distinguish one from the other. Fishing smacks she was sure of because they gave off a smell of diesel oil and fish. What she wanted, but hadn't yet seen, was a full-rigged sailing ship. She could see herself now, standing by the mast, with her long hair streaming in the nor'-nor'-west wind, and her father in blue blazer and white slacks giving orders to the crew as they headed out for the Great Gate and then south to the tropical islands of the Indies, where their newly decorated plantation mansion awaited them.

A flock of geese splashed up the bank from the river, paused to take stock of themselves and then made their way primly across the grass to the whitewashed farmhouse. Higher up, a heron stared glassily at the two girls before returning to his long, patient contemplation of the slowly moving water.

The splendid, full-rigged sailing ship vanished as Bridie watched John stowing away the picnic basket in his father's battered estate car. Why should such nice people as Uncle Graham and Aunt Mary be so poor? Why couldn't they have a splendid white sports car like her father's? No, no, no! She mustn't think of that now. Anything but that. Boats were safe. She lifted a rug off the grass and handed it to John.

"When you're a famous Harley Street specialist, will you have a boat of your own—I mean a ship?" She corrected herself hastily, still not quite sure which word to use. "You know—a clean-lined ship with white sails billowing in the wind." She liked the sound of that.

"Correction." John went on with his task. "For Harley Street specialist, read ordinary G.P."

"Why?"

"Because I don't want to be a specialist, in Harley Street or anywhere else. An ordinary G.P. That's what I want to be," John answered. At least, it's all I'm cut out for, he thought; he'd had wild ambitions when he was Kenneth's age, but now he knew his limitations. "With any luck I shall become an ordinary doctor, in an ordinary little village somewhere in the Western Highlands, and I'll have an ordinary rowing boat with a pair of ordinary oars so that I can go fishing on the nearest loch on my afternoon off once a month."

"I shall save up my money and buy you an outboard motor," Kenneth declared.

"What will you call your boat?" Bridie asked.

John looked at her speculatively. The more you gave her, the more she wanted, he thought.

"What'll I call my little rowing boat with two oars?" he repeated, very conscious of Bridie's demanding gaze.

"And an outboard motor when I'm rich," Kenneth reminded him.

"I must have notice of that question. Get in, all of you. Bridie in the front."

She was in the front when we came here, Sheena's glance told him. It isn't fair, because we see so little of you now.

John helped his sister into a back seat, gave her a conspiratorial wink, and watched her face clear. She's a nice kid, he thought, but she ought to consider herself more: she can be hurt so easily. At the back of his mind was the uncomfortable thought that he himself had just been guilty of trading on that very good nature.

"How long will it take you to get rich, Kenneth?" he asked, as they set off along the old causeway for the main road back to Oban.

"I reckon to be a millionaire by the time I'm twenty-two," Kenneth answered in an off-hand tone. "Big Business, you know."

"You haven't by any chance settled on the kind of Big Business that will make you rich so quickly?"

"Well, I did think of building a luxury hotel on Harris or somewhere, and setting up a fleet of fast ships for shark hunting, but the trouble is that you really need capital for that kind of thing."

John and Sheena groaned loudly.

"I thought Calum had knocked that idea on the head," Sheena said.

"What will you call your boat?" Bridie demanded petulantly. They'd no right to forget about her, to talk about islands she'd never been to, fishermen she'd never met.

"Kate is rather a nice name," John said, deciding he might as well give in now as later.

"But you like Bridie better. That's what you said when you met me off the train in Edinburgh and took me out to tea." She was trying to tell him that the English Kate and the Scottish Bridie were two different girls—or could be, with the right encouragement.

"Yes, we all think that Bridie suits you," John agreed, "and when I get a boat, I shall call it Bridie, after you."

Satisfied at last, Bridie stared ahead at the forests of Kilmichael and distant peaks of Ben Cruachan silhouetted against the darkening sky.

One by one the pale stars appeared, looking down on mountains and forests, glens and passes, moors and fields, searching out the sad remains of earlier peoples: plundered burial mounds built of stone and covered with turf; rings of standing stones, their significance now forgotten; flat rocks pecked with circles and pitted with hollows; splendid medieval crosses by unknown craftsmen; elaborate tombstones to commemorate the chieftains of clans, their glory long since departed, and a castle shell which spoke of pride and greed and a lust for power which still remained today.

As they climbed the last hill, Sheena cleared her window and looked down with a little sigh of pure happiness at the blaze of lights from the hotels and street lamps outlining the bay of Oban and stretching to the floodlit tower above. Lights marked the position of vessels anchored in the Sound or tied up in the harbours; they pin-pointed the farms and hamlets on the island of Kerrera and flashed their warning signals from the distant lighthouses.

"What's happening?" Bridie asked suddenly.

Whistling softly, John glanced into his mirror, slowed down and pulled onto the grass verge behind a line of parked cars whose occupants were clambering out and staring across at the night sky above Morvern.

"The Northern Lights," he exclaimed, getting out himself.

"The Merry Dancers," Kenneth cried, joining him.

Around them people murmured and exchanged awed comments as they stared up at the great cone of soaring, pulsating rays of light. Crimson and purple, green and azure, the bright streamers quivered and glowed, stretching and soaring upwards through the stars to an amber crown. Spellbound and silent now, the onlookers watched until the splendid colours began to fade a little, to dissolve and then reform, so that now the whole of the northern sky was red. Blood red.

"Fantastic," John muttered.

"They danced like this the night St Columba died on Iona," Kenneth said, "and the monks thought it was the angels carrying his soul to Heaven."

"It's a lovely idea," Sheena said slowly. "But people must have been terribly superstitious in those days, mustn't they?" She'd seen the lights on at least half a dozen occasions, and though none had been as splendid as this, each time she'd experienced the same peculiar blend of fear and attraction. It was as though they belonged to another, pagan world, possessing a force which could destroy unless it was accepted, obeyed, worshipped.

What nonsense she was thinking.

"I've an idea I'd have been superstitious if I'd lived when Columba did," Kenneth confessed.

"I'm sure we all should," John said, in a very matter-of-fact tone. "Take all natural phenomena—thunder, lightning, hurricanes, earthquakes—the lot. You can understand primitive people being frightened of them because they didn't know what caused them, but they did know they brought death and destruction.

"But quite soon they must have realized that the Northern Lights were like rainbows and shooting stars—mysterious but harmless."

Harmless? What made him think of that time on Mull when he was only a little boy and Sheena a baby in her pram? His grandmother and Calum had been talking about a variety of uninteresting (to him, at any rate) subjects, and then he'd caught the words "Merry Dancers", and listened because he liked the sound of them.

"When they turn blood red, bad luck is sure to follow," his grand-mother had said, and Calum had grunted and sucked at his old, smelly pipe.

"Blood red and dancing in the sky is a bad omen," he agreed. "A very bad omen."

John smiled at the memory, feeling justifiably superior. There was no room for superstitions, however old or quaint, in his clinical, aseptic world of medicine.

No doubt Calum would be standing at the door of his cottage at this moment, looking up at the sky and shaking his head. "A very bad omen," he'd be muttering. And when that bad-tempered pig of his got loose yet again and bolted down to the road to frighten the wits out of some harmless walkers, Iona-bound, it would all be the fault of the Merry Dancers, and would have nothing to do with the fact that Calum should have repaired the sty years ago.

Now he came to think about it, it was very convenient being able to shuffle off your own mistakes on a natural phenomenon which couldn't answer back. Perhaps education wasn't such a good thing after all. Or did he mean civilization? Well, whichever it was, today you were left with no one to blame but yourself.

Mistakes and the blame for them reminded him of Bridie, and he glanced at her profile, seeing the wrapt, far-away look as she gazed up at the now dimming lights. Yes, he thought with quiet confidence, Jennifer Nicholson had been right to send her daughter to his family. They could help her—they, and this land of Argyll which they so loved, and Mull and Iona and the islands of the Hebrides.

He could not see the muscle which twitched on the other side of Bridie's mouth. Only Kenneth was aware of that and of its significance, but it had been a long day, and now he was tired. He had no energy left even for himself. If Bridie wanted to go off into her dream world again, then she'd just have to go.

# 2 Calum of Mull

"WHAT WAS that you said, Bridie?" With a smile Mary MacDonald turned from her dreamy contemplation of the rapidly receding pier, with its red-roofed shipping offices and dwindling, waving holiday-makers, to give her attention to the girl beside her.

"I said you never get angry." Bridie had to raise her voice to make herself heard above the noise of the car ferry and its passengers, the sound of the white, churning waters and the shrieks of the ever-hungry seagulls. "And neither does Sheena," she continued happily. It was marvellous having her aunt all to herself, being treated with such kindness and affection, having her opinions sought, her queries answered. "Of course, Sheena's very like you. But the boys are different, aren't they?"

"Yes, the boys are different. In some ways they take after their grand-father, an ambitious, fiery tempered man." John was ambitious, she thought, but he was learning to recognize his limitations—or would do, before he qualified. Kenneth of course, was still a child, forever chang-ing his mind and opinions.

Still smiling, she looked back to the mainland. No matter how often they made the crossing from Oban to Mull she never tired of watching the splendid sweep of the bay with its semi-circle of hotels in varying shades of grey and red and white, and the stone houses climbing the wooded hillside to the double coronet of McCaig's Tower. McCaig's Folly, some people called it, sneering at it as a pale imitation of the Colosseum of Rome. Mary loved it. She had never been abroad—and she included England in that term—but she was convinced that there was nowhere to equal the beauty of the Western Highlands or the islands of the Hebrides.

"Daddy was just like Uncle Graham," Bridie said. "He was slimmer, but almost as tall, and very good-looking. He was more sociable than Uncle Graham, if you know what I mean. He loved going places and doing things. He liked people, lots of people; and he hated staying at home and doing nothing. He had to travel a great deal—all over Europe and America. And Asia too. And he always brought a present back for me. Always."

As Bridie talked of her father and herself and shot adoring glances at her aunt from time to time, Mary MacDonald decided that, no matter what the English doctors had said, sooner or later Bridie would simply have to accept both herself and her family as they really were; and, as far as she was concerned, it ought to be sooner, before Bridie rejected her mother completely and expected her aunt to fill the role.

This was something neither she nor her husband had dreamed of, that day they had comforted Jennifer Nicholson and said that of course her daughter could come and stay with them as long as she wanted.

Some of their friends said they were crazy: others thought the invitation was typical of the way the MacDonalds always responded to cries for help.

It wasn't as though Jenny was a close friend. Although Mary had read a lot about her in papers and magazines, she'd only met her twice.

The first time was when they were girls. Jenny's parents had rented the house next door to Mary's in Oban, for the summer holidays. The two girls had soon become friends, discovering an exciting, if tenuous, kinship in the fact that both possessed grandparents born on Barra, an island where everybody was reputed to be related to everyone else.

They vowed eternal friendship, as girls do, wrote regularly for a couple of months, exchanged Christmas cards, and finally forgot about each other.

It was just after Mary had become engaged to Graham that she opened her newspaper one morning to see a startlingly beautiful Jenny gazing out at her. It appeared that she was an actress in some repertory theatre, and had eloped with the handsome and popular radio and television personality, Simon Nicholson. Their marriage was delayed by the fact that Simon was already married.

Mary and Jenny met for the second time when Jenny brought Simon up to Oban for a holiday and stayed at the largest and most expensive, turreted hotel on the sea front. Jenny cooed over the energetic young John and the placid baby, Sheena, but failed to understand why her former friend could not hand her children over to friends and tear around the country with them in their new American car, or join them at their hotel for drinks and dinner and dancing.

Jenny and Simon spent one evening with the MacDonalds and talked wittily and entertainingly of the worlds of the theatre, television and the cinema. It made Mary realize what a quiet, uneventful life she led. For a day or two she envied Jenny, and then she forgot about her again.

When the distraught but still beautiful Jenny had come to them for help last Easter, Mary was convinced it was because of that first holiday they'd spent together—a holiday which, with the passing of the years, had grown more and more idyllic.

Was Jenny hoping that their daughters would be as happy together as they had been? If so, she was doomed to disappointment. Try as she might, Sheena could not bridge the eighteen-month gap between Bridie and herself, could find no common interest, no way of arousing any real enthusiasm in the withdrawn girl.

Kenneth was more successful, but how long he was prepared to put up with Bridie's moodiness, her constant demands for attention and reassurance, his mother did not know. She squashed herself against Bridie to allow a polite Australian to film Duart Castle, still grey and menacing, although it was long since the power of the Macleans had passed from Mull. Nearby, guide book in hand, an attractive young teacher was pointing out to her charges Lady's Rock, where one of the Macleans, tired of his wife, had abandoned her (unsuccessfully, as it turned out) to drown at high water. If Kenneth had been here Mary thought, he'd have told the teacher she was looking at the wrong rock altogether. Kenneth was a great one for getting other people's facts right.

"What tartan is that?" Bridie asked, as the ferry rolled a little in the swell and a portly, kilted man cannoned off an empty chair and gravely offered it his apologies.

"The Royal Stuart."

"Daddy used to wear a kilt. He was in the Black Watch, you know, and fought right through the War. He was wounded twice, and he was decorated at Buckingham Palace. I can remember him coming into my nursery with his kilt swinging, and lifting me up in his arms. 'Bridie,' he said—he was the only one who called me that: everyone else called me Kate, you know. 'Wish me luck, my bonnie Bridie,' he said. 'I'm off to fight for King and Country!' "

With one finger Mary turned the girl's face to hers and smiled gently; it wasn't difficult for her to recognize in this wild invention yet another —and quite unnecessary—bid for more love and attention.

"Now, Bridie, you know quite well you're making it all up as you go along. Your father was only a schoolboy during the War, and never was in the Army."

"Oh!"

Prepared from past experience for the girl's sullen anger, Mary ignored it completely, continuing to speak in the same gentle voice with the soft Highland lilt which Bridie found so attractive. "It's that Barra strain you've inherited from your great-great-grandmother O'Neill. People with Hebridean blood—the lucky ones, that is—just can't help imagining wonderful, fantastic, impossible stories. Hour after hour during the long winter nights the folk of Barra would gather round the peat fire for a *ceilidh,* and your great-great-grandmother O'Neill would repeat the old stories and make up new ones and no one could tell the difference, so gifted was she. But there was one thing she never did: she never got caught up in her own imagination."

Bridie's face glowed again.

"Dear Aunt Mary, I do love you so. I wish I could live with you always. I wish. . . ."

Bells rang stridently. Parents shouted to children to come and get ready, that they'd be at Craignure any minute now; and while carrier bags were being repacked, lost garments found and fathers retrieved from the bar, Mary led Bridie over to where the gangway would be hoisted, so that they could be first off the ferry.

At six feet two inches, with his thick grey hair and piercing blue eyes —a legacy from some Viking forebear—Graham MacDonald was easy to pick out among the crowd waiting on the pier.

"Good crossing?" he asked, seizing their cases, kissing his wife and smiling warmly at Bridie.

"Marvellous," Bridie answered, breaking into a trot as she tried to keep up with him. "I wanted it to go on for ever and ever."

They were in the car and away long before the coaches had filled up with holiday-makers bound for the Iona ferry or off on a circular tour of Mull.

"Did you have a rest, Mary?" Graham asked, as they drove through the wooded policies of the Victorian Torosay Castle.

"I did indeed. Bridie wouldn't let me do anything. She prepared the meals, washed up and did the housework. I've been quite spoiled."

Bridie glowed.

Poor Sheena, Mary thought. Each year she's looked forward to these three days alone with me while Graham and the boys got the cottage ready, but as soon as Bridie announced that she wanted to stay in Oban and look after me, Sheena agreed without demur and went off with the others. Perhaps it's time for her to assert herself a little more. Bridie can't expect to have things her own way all the time. Or can she?

The road skirted the shores of Loch Spelve and now sad-eyed seals basked where once the Macleans had beached their war galleys; on it twisted, following the bright Lussa through green bracken and fading heather to thread the Pass of Glen More. High up among the bleak hills a herd of deer sheltered from the wind, so still that Bridie took them for boulders or shadows until one moved and the whole herd followed, disappearing into a dark, narrow pass.

"Had you much to do in the cottage, Graham? Had the last tenants left it in order?"

"You don't really believe that Calum would let anyone leave unless the place was spick and span, do you? No, Sheena organized everything so efficiently there was hardly anything to do except lay in stocks of food."

"Is Calum a relative?" Bridie asked, thinking of how often his name seemed to crop up.

Graham looked startled.

"That must be the only idea that hasn't occurred to him—yet," he said.

"He's our nearest neighbour," Mary explained. "Years ago, when we bought the cottage and Graham decided to modernize and enlarge it, Calum was very interested. He knew everyone on Mull, and he knew how to get everything, from a fresh supply of exactly the right stone to a plumber and electrician."

"There was far more work to be done than I first realized," Graham admitted, "especially as I only had weekends and holidays and the children were too little to do anything except get in the way, so I asked Calum if he'd be interested in helping me. From that day, he was the master and I, the unwilling slave."

Mary laughed.

"What nonsense you talk, Graham. Just because he didn't always think you were right. You know you'd never have got the place finished without him."

"I agree with you there," her husband said, with much feeling. "If I'd got on the wrong side of Calum, he'd probably have invoked some of those malevolent pagan spirits which he talks about at great length and swears still exist in these parts, and they'd have brought the whole place crashing down round my ears."

"I never noticed you being unwilling to stop work and listen to his tales no matter how long they were," Mary commented. "How old do you think he is, Graham?"

"That, no one will ever know. Once, when—as he himself put it—he'd had a skinful, he told me that he could remember the day my great-grandfather was born in Dervaig."

"Goodness! What did you say?"

"Nothing. What could I say?"

"You could have tried: 'Why, Calum, you don't look a hundred and thirty to me!' " And they both laughed.

"See where the loch narrows there?" Graham said, aware that Bridie was quite uninterested in their reminiscences. "There used to be an old ford there. The road we've come along is new: before that, pilgrims had to go all the way round by the shores of Loch na Keal, on the far side of

Ben More, to get to the Ross and then sail over to Iona."

Bridie smiled and nodded, but the exhilaration she had experienced on the ferry was ebbing now as she looked from the derelict houses at the foot of barren hills on one side, to the grey water and grey mists on the other. What on earth was she going to do with herself here for a whole, long month?

Her dismay increased as the car slowed down and they turned off the road, bumping along a rough track to a plain, slate-roofed cottage, built for protection against the foot of a steep, heather-clad hill. Outbuildings on the right had been converted into bedrooms connected with each other and the cottage by a narrow passage. A back door opened out from this passage on to a small yard, where the car was parked.

The front door was flanked on one side by a flourishing fuchsia and on the other by a drooping rowan tree.

"The guardian of the cottage," Graham said, well aware of Bridie's thoughts. It was only when she retreated into her world of make-believe that her face became expressionless, except for that nervous tic. Better have her disapproving than that, he thought philosophically.

"What do you mean, Uncle Graham?"

"Our rowan tree. The mountain ash. Puts the fear of death into witches, wicked fairies, hobgoblins, foul fiends and all things that go bump in the night. None of them dares cross the threshold of any cottage where it grows."

"Or can harm anyone who carries a sprig," his wife added. "At least that's what Calum says. He once told me that he'd never walk through Pennygowan Churchyard at midnight without a rowan twig in his pocket, and when I asked him why he wanted to walk through any churchyard at midnight, he just gave me a pitying look and shuffled off."

"I should think so too," Graham said. "You should know by now that Calum is always right. He never argues, never explains. You take him as he is, or not at all."

"I'm sure that's so, Graham. But what is he?"

"That's a question I've often asked myself. Sometimes I think he's the last representative of another breed of men. I do know this, though —when he goes, Mull will be the poorer."

As he got out of the car, the back door of the cottage opened and Kenneth dashed out, wiping his mouth with the back of his hand.

"Thirty seconds early," he announced. "Well druv, Pa. And dinner's ready."

"Bangers and mash?" his mother asked, ruffling his dark, untidy hair, so that he knew he'd been right not to waste time combing it that morning.

"We persuaded him to be really daring for once," John said, coming forward to help his father with the cases. "In your honour, Bridie."

"It's a special broth," Kenneth announced importantly, "made with potatoes and onions and turnips and barley and—wait for it —venison."

"Calum?" Graham asked, looking at his elder son.

"How did you guess? Probably poached too."

"I wonder if we'll all have to go to jail, or if the magistrates will settle for me."

"Don't worry, Pa," Kenneth said reassuringly. "I expect the magistrates are all having venison too." Suddenly he saw Bridie. "Glory! What have you done to your hair?"

"I had a colour rinse," she answered lightly. She'd rehearsed her reply the previous evening so that it would sound absolutely natural, but, to her chagrin, her aunt had been too busy packing and closing up the Oban house to notice the change from brown to honey blonde. Or had she noticed and deliberately made no comment?

"You dyed it?" Kenneth said incredulously. "What on earth for?"

He makes it sound as though I've committed some unforgivable sin, Bridie thought, and not for anything would she have admitted to the secret satisfaction she was feeling at the moment. She'd shake them out of their plain, Presbyterian way of life. They were all looking at her now. She was glad she'd bought this pale blue trouser suit yesterday.

"Why did you do it?" Kenneth demanded aggressively. He stood there, bare-footed, in his faded jeans and mended shirt (he was rather proud of the way he'd sewn up that tear underneath the right arm) thinking what fun they'd had getting everything ready for their mother, and the minute Bridie showed up she had to spoil things by being all dolled up as though she'd expected to stay at that new posh hotel for millionaires.

"I think the colour suits Bridie," Sheena said, from the doorway where she had just appeared. "I expect it was that colour when you were a little girl. And I do like your trouser suit. I'm going to try to make myself one this winter."

"I think Bridie looks very nice too," Mary said, giving her daughter a warm kiss. "Will you take her across to her room and see she has everything she needs? And then come back and tell me all that's happened here."

It hadn't been worth it, Bridie thought afterwards. For a moment she'd held their attention and then they'd linked together—one family tolerating her, the outsider, because they were nice people.

Nice, but poor. This cottage they were so proud of was nothing but a watered-down version of their shabby terrace house in Oban. Aunt Mary admitted that most of the furniture had been bought cheaply at sales and auctions, as though a few coats of paint could transform a scratched dressing-table, an old rocking-chair, a creaking wardrobe and an iron bedstead into anything like her own modern Scandinavian furniture, or a tatty rag mat compare with her fitted carpet.

"I'll wash up," Sheena said, when there was nothing left of the venison stew, and the apple tart which her mother had brought across with her had disappeared too.

"Oh, no, you won't," John contradicted. "It's Little Horror's turn, and he's not wriggling out of it again."

Kenneth, who had been making his way to the door in what he hoped was an unobtrusive manner, halted and turned.

"When I'm a millionaire," he announced, speaking apparently to the ceiling, "I shall have disposable crockery of the very best Crown Derby and solid silver cutlery, and everything will be thrown away after every meal so that there will never, never be any washing up at all."

"Splendid!" his father said, as everyone laughed. "But until that happy day, it's into the kitchen with you, my lad."

"I'll help you, Kenneth," Bridie said, hoping this magnanimous offer would be appreciated by all the family, but they seemed more concerned with what they should do and where they should go that afternoon and whether or not it was going to rain.

Kenneth, however, was most profuse in his thanks, and together they had the dishes cleared away and stacked in the sink just as the others set off for their walk.

"You get started, Bridie," Kenneth said, thoughtfully handing her an apron. "I'll be back in a sec," and he disappeared. A moment later she saw him running down the drive, whistling triumphantly, throwing an old tennis ball up in the air and catching it in various contorted positions.

At first she was so angry she decided the dishes could wait until he came back; then she was hurt that he could play such a mean trick on her—she had conveniently forgotten the trick she had played on him when they went to Dunadd. Finally she shrugged her shoulders and set to work, weaving a dream world about her in which she lived with her father in a New York penthouse overlooking the river, and barbecued T-bone steaks on the roof garden before setting off for their country home on Long Island.

How quiet the cottage was, she thought, hanging up the tea towel and returning, metaphorically at any rate, from riches to rags. How mean of them to clear off and leave her alone in this desolate spot. She drifted through the rooms and out of the front door, to lean disconsolately against the rowan and watch the little waves of the sea loch surge forward among the shells and pebbles and retreat again, hissing softly. The wind blew a pliant branch against her cheek and, irritated, she knocked it aside. The next time the shiny leaves brushed her face, rather than move, she snapped off the end of the branch. Beadbonny ash, she muttered fingering the brilliant orange-red berries as she tried to recall the lines her uncle had quoted at lunch. There was something about dew and braes and then—yes—

> Wiry heathpacks, flitches of fern,
> And the beadbonny ash that sits over the burn.

Beadbonny ash . . . she liked the sound of the words and the image they conjured up. Her father had always thought that one day she'd be a famous poet because of this feeling for words that just came naturally to her. One day he'd sent some of her work up to a famous publisher and he'd said—No, no, no. She wouldn't start dreaming again.

Quite suddenly she knew she was no longer alone. Something had come, softly, silently through the yard and was standing behind her, watching her. Something that gave off a most unpleasant smell.

Slowly she turned her head. A huge pink creature was staring at her with sly, bloodshot eyes: dried dung was caked on the coarse bristles of its neck and shoulders and two yellow, curling tusks protruded from the crooked, salivating mouth.

Terrified, she tried to scream for help, but no sound came from her parted lips. All she had to do was to take a couple of steps backwards and slam the door to gain the safety of the cottage, but she was as rooted to the ground as the rowan against which she was leaning.

"It's the Evil One himself that is in you, Obadiah," an angry voice cried, "and one of these days it is no more fine pigs that you will be siring, but it is all cut up you will be, in neat slices for my breakfast." Breathing heavily, an old man walked round the corner of the cottage and began to scratch the animal with the stick he was carrying. His trousers, which had obviously been made for a much fatter man than he, were tied up with rope and string, while his shirt revealed more of his dirty vest than it concealed.

"And will the Major be being at home now?"

The Major? What Major, Bridie thought wildly, as beside her the creature grunted and snuffled in ecstasy, as the stick scratched its hideous hide. Of course. Uncle Graham. He'd been in the Army, although she'd never heard him called Major before.

"There is some peats for the fire, see here. Coal is good enough for me, but for visitors peats is nice and makes them feel like us, which they are not and never will be. But peats is nice, and just when I am leaving, what should happen but Obadiah here is smitten with loneliness and breaks down his wall and comes too, and me with no hands but these two, and them on the handles of the barrow to keep it from running away with the peats and myself into the bargain. 'Come back, Obadiah!' I am calling, but the deafness of convenience is upon him and on he runs.

"But when I come here, I am scarcely believing my eyes, for there you are, standing so calm and staring down at Obadiah with the look of authority so that you might be a goddess from the old forgotten days, and there is Obadiah, recognizing the look and standing still with not a muscle moving, and him the terror of all Mull."

The look of authority? Bridie wondered if she had heard aright. Did he really think that? Couldn't he see how frightened she was? Was he laughing at her?

"Standing there so calm," the old man repeated, "and not a word from you who you might be."

At last she found her voice.

"Me? I'm Bridie Nicholson, and I'm the great-great-granddaughter of Brigid O'Neill of Barra." And what on earth had made her answer like that, she wondered, dragging in a relative she hadn't known existed until she came to stay with the MacDonalds.

"Aye. Bridie O'Neill of Barra. That explains why I will be knowing your face well, and you a stranger."

"Bridie!" Flushed and breathless, Sheena appeared round the curve of the road, waving her hand as she hurried up to the cottage. "I'm terribly sorry, Bridie. Kenneth is a beast. I've just seen him down on the shore and he told me he'd cleared off and left you on your own. Are you all right?"

"Of course," Bridie answered stiffly. "Why shouldn't I be? I'm not a child, you know." But before she had finished, Sheena had turned to the old man with a warm smile.

"Hello, Calum. I see you've met our Bridie."

"Aye, princess, and Obadiah is meeting her too. Like an arrow he is flying past me, and me slow in my old age and burdened with peats and full of fear on account of his anger. But all the time he is knowing her for what she is, and recognizing the power of her eye so that he is standing by her as docile as a new-born lamb. Is it not the bare truth that I am telling, Bridie of Barra?"

Avoiding Sheena's eyes, Bridie nodded. It was, perhaps, the truth as Calum saw it, and she was quite prepared to take credit even where it wasn't due. She knew that before very long she would believe it herself.

"Well, Bridie may be able to subdue Obadiah by looking at him, Calum, but I certainly can't. Frankly, I'm terrified of him. I do wish you'd put his harness on."

"Anything at all to please my little princess," Calum agreed, forgetting his offer immediately as he launched into a long and involved story about Obadiah's sire, a boar of incredible proportions and notorious ill temper—characteristics which, Sheena declared, Obadiah had not only inherited, but had increased.

At the last mention of his name, Obadiah raised his head and grunted, and Sheena jumped back in alarm.

"It's all right," Bridie said. "It's the music. He can hear it. But who can be playing a harp here?"

"I can't hear any music," Sheena said, looking around. With a loud snorting, the boar struggled to his feet and made for the road, deaf to Calum's orders, first in English and then in Gaelic.

Unwinding the rope from his waist, Calum hurried after the beast with a speed surprising for an old man, caught up with him just as he was about to cross the road, and harangued him in Gaelic as he adjusted the harness of his own invention.

"Can you understand what he's saying?" Bridie asked.

Sheena shook her head.

"Not a word. He offered to teach me, but Daddy put his foot down. He said I'd learn all I need at school. I think Kenneth's picked up a few expressions he daren't use at home, though."

"He's listening to the music and the singing, Sheena," Bridie persisted, as they made their way down to the road. "Just look at the way he's turning his head."

A passing cyclist waved to the girls and Sheena waved back.

"The only reason Obadiah is turning his head is because he wants to use that right tusk of his to rip open Iain Murray's leg. Believe me, Bridie, that beast is dangerous. Reallly dangerous."

"He may be dangerous at other times, but at present he's listening to the woman along there." Now they could see past the bend in the road, and Bridie pointed to the group round the driftwood fire by the side of the loch.

"What is it that you are seeing, Bridie of Barra?" Calum asked softly.

"Those people—gypsies, I suppose. The old woman singing, and playing the harp—"

"*Clarsach* is being its name."

"—*Clarsach*, and the tall man and the dwarf, and someone covered with rugs on the couch. I'm sure I've seen them all before, but I can't think where."

Dismayed, Sheena stared from Bridie to Calum. It was the first time Bridie had spoken to her of an imaginary world quite unconnected with the father she had idolized, and she didn't know what to do. Why was Calum staring at Bridie like that? Was he about to come out with something forthright and blunt that might push her farther back into her dream world, undo any good that might have been achieved since she came to them, withdrawn and uncommunicative by day, screaming out in terror as the nightmares gripped her when she fell asleep? It was a long time now since Bridie had had a nightmare, and she was beginning to join in their family life. No, Calum mustn't do anything to upset her. Then she remembered something.

"Calum. Why did you say *clarsach*?"

"Because it is the small harp, the old one, that the Hag is playing."

"You mean you can see these people? Hear some kind of music?" Once, when she was a child, she'd reproved him gravely for calling someone a hag, but he'd said that in the Gaelic it meant an old woman of some authority who was greatly respected by some and much feared by others.

"Of course he can. Look, Sheena!" Bridie grasped her arm and pointed along the shore. "There."

Amazed, Sheena stared at the distant group. How was it that until now she hadn't heard the harp music which spoke of the Other-world, of the magic that is woven strand by strand into the tapestry of present life? What threat or promise had been offered to the old gods for this song which could both waken the dead and lull the living to sleep? Listen long enough, the Hag and the *clarsach* promised, and you will have the understanding of the speech of birds and beasts. Surrender to us, and you will learn the purpose of suffering and pain, and with knowledge will come tranquillity.

A large, gleaming car with Swiss registration plates drove past, windows open and radio playing, and pulled up farther down the road, hiding the group. Excited German voices mingled with the radio as the driver opened his door. Bearded and bald, his *embonpoint* almost concealed by the expert tailoring of his light grey suit, he adjusted his ciné camera to record this gift of a scene which the gods had cast—almost literally—in his path, and then with a regal wave he stepped back into his car and drove off.

"Well!" Suddenly realizing what had happened, Sheena forgot the music and stared helplessly after the car.

"How happy he is!" Calum said, his eyes gleaming. "How he will boast when he returns to his rich home in his rich city and there we are, forever, part of his moving picture—the poor old swineherd of Mull with his tethered boar and his poor but beautiful daughters beside him, or is it wives that you are, me being so young and handsome?"

Sheena began to laugh, but Bridie was furious. A foreigner to mistake her for a . . . a peasant! She saw Calum looking at her slyly and knew he was laughing at her. He'd been laughing at her before, she thought when he pretended she had subdued his wretched pig just by looking at it.

Once, long ago, she had laughed just as Sheena was laughing now. Her anger began to fade.

"Will two handsome princes disguise themselves and come along and ask for our hands in marriage?" she asked. It wasn't very funny but she thought there was a gleam of something like approval in Calum's eyes, and suddenly they were all laughing, joyfully, helplessly, at the thought of the story it would make when it was told and retold later.

"They've gone!" Bridie exclaimed, staring at the now deserted shore. Laughter fled. "Where? And how? There's no sign of them anywhere. Even if they'd had a car . . . and what happened to the fire?"

Far away a seabird wailed mournfully.

Looking down, Bridie discovered that she was still clutching the twig she had broken off as she stood beside the ash tree—the beadbonny ash. It had a comforting feel about it which had, she assured herself, absolutely nothing to do with superstition.

Calum was eyeing her curiously. She knew this and didn't want to look up, but she seemed to have lost her will power. She stared at the network of folds and creases which crossed the brown forehead and radiated from the outer corners of his eyes; she saw the thick, straggling eyebrows, the long lashes and—helpless now—she stared into the grey-green eyes that were the colour of the Atlantic waters and were far more perilous. . . .

"Would you like to walk along the shore and look for shells? We've found some very pretty ones here."

Sheena's voice seemed to come from a long way off, and Bridie had to make an even greater effort than usual to wrench herself out of her dream world. "Shells? Yes . . . of course. Of course."

Dazed, she looked round. This was the second time she'd entered and left her secret world without realizing what she was doing or remembering what had happened. There had been a first time, but when it was she couldn't recall. It wasn't really important just now.

"How did they get there?" she asked, pointing to Calum and his boar as they disappeared over the top of the hill, behind the MacDonalds' cottage.

"Walked," Sheena answered. "I suppose," she added uncertainly. "Now I come to think of it, I don't remember him saying good-bye or leaving us or anything. How odd!" She looked up but the man and beast were out of sight now. She too could remember nothing of the group by the side of the loch, of the harp music or the singing.

"Perhaps they flew," Bridie suggested gravely.

"I wouldn't put it past them," Sheena answered, equally gravely. "I wouldn't put anything past Calum and Obadiah."

"That great fat, pink pig with wings," Bridie said. And suddenly she began to giggle as she had done when she was a child and was captivated by the utter absurdity of the idea.

"And Calum's trousers flapping in the wind so that he'd probably not need wings at all," Sheena added, and together they laughed until the tears rolled down their cheeks, and when at last they sobered up, Bridie knew that she loved Sheena.

She wanted to explain how much she admired the other's gentleness and unselfishness, how she was the kind of sister she'd always longed for: she wanted to tell Sheena the truth about everything, but especially about that terrible night . . . her birthday . . . when she had waited. . . .

It wouldn't be easy, but she could do it. With Sheena's help she could do it. She began to rehearse it silently.

I'd planned it for months. Prawn cocktails, and roast chicken with little sausages and stuffing and peas, ice cream for Daddy and cheese and biscuits for Jenny.

Jenny. Your mother would never want you to call her by her Christian name, would she? Mine insisted on it. Awfully nicely, of course. It made us closer. More like sisters. But I didn't want her to be a sister. I wanted a mother, Sheena. I wanted to go on calling her Mummy. I often do, to myself. Mummy.

Did I tell you I had candles? And linen napkins folded in bishops' mitres?

But they didn't come. I waited, but they didn't come.

It was after midnight when Daddy turned up. I could tell from his face they'd been quarrelling again and had forgotten all about me. On my birthday.

Daddy pretended he hadn't—forgotten, I mean. I don't remember what excuse he gave. He'd been drinking. He wasn't drunk but he'd been drinking. He said he'd come to take me for a night-ride because I was the only one who loved him. I'm not making that up, Sheena. He really did say it.

So I just had to go with him.

When we got to the motorway he kept on saying, "Want to go faster, Katie?" and I'd say "Yes," because that was what he needed—me to admire him.

He was laughing when the crash came. Then he wasn't laughing any more. He wasn't Daddy any more. He wasn't . . . anyone at all . . . any more.

"Bridie," Sheena cried suddenly, "there's Mummy and Daddy coming along the shore. Let's go and see if they've found anything. Mummy's the luckiest beachcomber in the world. She finds sea treasures without even looking for them. I remember once. . . ."

The moment was lost.

Love ebbed, and with it courage, and Bridie, almost sick with despair, knew that she would never forgive Sheena for failing her at the very moment she had found enough courage to ask for the help she needed so desperately.

# 3  Iona of my Heart

THE NORTH-WEST WIND hurled the rain against the cottage and pried into the small deep-set windows; it chased the torn clouds over the hill tops and through the passes, whipped the surface of Loch Scridain into angry waves and snatched at the spindrift, scattering it over the Ross road.

How much longer could she stand life on this dreary island, Bridie asked herself. No one realized how hard she had tried to return to a normal life. No one ever thought to ask why she should live alone, unloved on a cold, wet island when she could be so happy and cherished in a world of her own creation.

No one really cared about her. Oh, they did their best. Sheena had been the first to try to lure her out of the protection of her bedroom. Would Bridie care to join them? She and John and their father were going out on the loch with Calum.

Whether it was to fish, collect lobster pots, or simply row across to visit someone on the opposite shore, Bridie didn't bother to find out. To be tossed up and down in a little boat on a rough sea, with the rain driving against you—she couldn't imagine anything more horrible, she told Sheena, and she watched with incredulity as the oilskin-clad figures departed, laughing and joking as though they really enjoyed being out in such weather.

Kenneth came along next, bringing a small notebook and a large box full of coloured stones. His plan for becoming a millionaire (by building super hotels for shark fishermen) abandoned through lack of capital, he had now decided to make his fortune as a dealer in precious stones. Amethyst, opal, cairngorm, topaz, agate, beryl and jasper—the names fell off his tongue with rather more assurance than accuracy as he invited Bridie to inspect first one stone and then another.

Of course they had to be cut and polished, he explained, and while he hadn't got either the tools or the experience yet, he didn't think it would take him long to acquire both. Now, actually, what he had come to say was that he knew a highly secret place only a few miles away at the bottom of the cliffs on the southern shore of the Ross, where there were magnificent sapphires and diamonds embedded in the rocks, and he was prepared to take Bridie there and lend her a hammer and chisel to pry out her finds.

"Today?" she asked. "In this rain?"

"It's not raining much. Come on, Bridie. I'll make you a director of my company. You can have an office of your own and twenty-five per cent of the profits."

But not even the offer of a fitted carpet, electric typewriter and fifty per cent of the profits could induce Bridie to show the slightest interest in the expedition.

After Kenneth had flung out of the room, rejected and disappointed, she wished she'd been kinder. She was very polite when her aunt came to see if she'd like to learn how to knit a Fair Isle pullover like Sheena's. It was very kind of her aunt, but no thank you, she just didn't like knitting and she was perfectly happy reading in her own room. She did read a little, but most of the day she spent with her father in an imaginary and romantic island of the West Indies.

After supper she allowed them to persuade her to join in a game of Monopoly, but it wasn't long before buying property reminded her of the collection of postcards she possessed of all kinds of hotels, from five-star modern ones in England, luxury motels with swimming pools in America, exotic palaces in Spain, to little family concerns in Turkey and Egypt, where the food was out of this world.

"Everywhere Daddy went on location, he always sent me a card," she explained airily. "And every time he went to a new country he brought me back a doll dressed in the national costume. I've got the most fantastic collection. I expect some day I'll leave it to the British Museum or somewhere like that. It must be worth a fortune."

They listened courteously and agreed that she was very lucky, but when Kenneth cleared his throat—a sign that he was about to start an argument—a look from his mother silenced him. After a pause to make sure that Bridie had finished talking, Sheena picked up the dice and amidst much laughter, went straight to jail.

In the end, Kenneth was the winner.

"It's an omen. A good omen," he declared, counting his money like a miser. "I wonder if it would be an idea to start a Know Your Highlands and Islands Company. Guided tours by road, rail, air and steamer to places famous in legend and history."

"Anything that'll get you to learn some history or even open a book occasionally would be a good idea," his father said.

It was raining when they went to bed.

It was still raining when Bridie woke the next morning. At eleven she made coffee for everyone and volunteered to take John's upstairs, to the room where he was studying.

His "Come in," was not particularly welcoming and he didn't bother to look up when she opened the door.

"I brought your elevenses," she announced brightly.

"Thanks. Put it down somewhere."

She did so, and waited until at last he raised his head.

"I haven't anything to read, John. Would you mind if I borrowed one of your books?"

"Be my guest." He waved one hand in the direction of the bookcase. "Top shelf—medical books—won't interest you. Try any of the others." He returned to his work, and, accustomed to studying against a noisy background, promptly forgot about her.

When, considerably later, he glanced up, he found her engrossed in a popular illustrated history of medicine which he'd bought second-hand when he was still at school. Shouldn't be anything there to give her nightmares, he thought, but when he rose to make certain, she replaced it hastily on the shelf and grabbed *The Life of St Columba*.

"Oh, yes," he said, taking the book from her and looking at the fly-leaf. "That's Kenneth's. A relic from his pre-millionaire days, when he was going to live on Iona, be a monk, and reform the world. It was", he added, "a trying time for everyone. He used to make a list of all our faults and pray in a very loud voice each evening that he, with the help of Columba, would make us see the error of our ways.

"I think his enthusiasm began to wane when he tried to convert Calum—an old pagan, if ever there was one. I forget what happened exactly. I think Kenneth told him about Columba being caught in a storm on a loch, and commanding the storm to cease."

"And did it?" Bridie asked, eager to delay her departure as long as possible.

"According to Columba's biographers, it did. Anyway Calum wasn't impressed. He offered to do the reverse. It was a fine, calm day and he offered to whistle up a west wind and a storm too."

"And what happened?" Her interest was genuine now.

"He whistled. In less than an hour a force eight gale was blowing."

Bridie thought this over.

"Do you think he'd heard the radio weather forecast?"

"People don't think much of those forecasts around here. It's what Calum says that they go by, and speaking for myself, I've never known him be far wrong."

"This Columba," Bridie said hastily, as John showed signs of returning to his work, "he was the one who came here from Ireland to convert the Picts and Celts, wasn't he? Well, if they were simple people, and he was clever—because he was a prince and the monks had educated him—he'd probably know things like when the wind was going to change, or be able to tell from the clouds if it was going to rain, and that would impress the Picts and they'd decide to become Christians like him."

"True enough," John agreed, thinking what a rational and intelligent child she appeared to be now. "But don't forget, Columba would be up against some pretty stiff opposition from the pagan priests, who were probably quite good at impressing the locals with their own weather forecasts, to say nothing of the odd miracle here and there."

"Druids?" Bridie's eyes sparkled. "Long white beards and golden sickles and mistletoe and burning victims alive in wicker cages?"

"Who on earth told you that rubbish?" When he saw the way her face fell he wished he'd been more tactful.

"I didn't know it was rubbish. Daddy was in a film once. They shot it in Wales. He was the Arch-Druid and he led the fight against the Romans. He was marvellous. The Romans captured him and wanted him to betray his people. But he wouldn't. There was blood, because he was wounded."

John didn't need to be a medical student to appreciate the significance of that twitching muscle at the corner of Bridie's mouth.

"Bridie, I've had an idea. Instead of reading about Columba, how about going to Iona and seeing his church for yourself?"

"Just the two of us?"

"Just the two of us."

"Oh, John, I'd love to. But it's still pouring. Look at it."

"Despair not, maiden," he said in histrionic tones. "Let me don my Druid's cap and forecast that ere we set foot on the white sands of Iona, the rain will have ceased and the sun will be shining."

"Do you really think so?" She was begging for reassurance.

"I have spoken!" Smiling, he shed his prophetic role. "How long will it take you to get yourself and a picnic ready?"

"Quarter of an hour. Less."

John glanced at his watch.

"I'll give you half an hour. Put on those shoes you bought in Oban and that fetching red weatherproof coat and hat, and we'll get the coach just outside the cottage. Off with you now."

How different the child looked when she laughed, he thought. What a change already from the sullen, overweight girl he'd met at Edinburgh station at Easter and taken out for tea. Every attempt at conversation had been blocked with a whispered "No, thank you," or "I don't know," or a blank stare. He'd been calling her Kate because that was

how her mother referred to her, when he noticed the initials on her case.
B.K.G.

"What does the B stand for?" he asked.

"Brigid."

"You never get called that?"

"No."

"Pity. It's an old Hebridean name. On Barra they shorten it to
Bridie." He watched her lips move as she whispered the name to herself.

"Can people change their names?" It was the first question she had
asked.

"Nothing easier. You'd like to be Bridie while you're staying with my
folks in Oban?"

"Please—oh, please."

And Bridie she was.

"It's a tremendous step psychologically," John explained to his
mother later. "It means she's getting ready to abandon the Kate side of
her, along with all that happened in London. Once she really settles
down to being Bridie, she'll be ready to come to terms with herself and
with life."

When he had returned to Oban a week ago, he had been struck by the
tremendous improvement in Bridie's health and appearance, but so far
she had eluded every attempt, direct or indirect, either to accept or to
discuss the past.

As things had turned out he thought today might offer the ideal con-
ditions for him to gain her trust and confidence: perhaps, surrounded by
the peace and serenity of Iona, he might succeed where others had
failed.

"I don't think you'd have made a very good Druid," Bridie said as
they took their seats on the coach, but she was laughing as she spoke.
Two girls at the front had muttered "Smashing!" when they saw John,
and Bridie immediately experienced a possessive pride as well as some
other pleasant emotion she didn't want to analyse.

"We're still on Mull," John reminded her, watching as she cleared
the misted window and looked out as the rain lashed down on the huddled stone houses of Bunessan. Someone behind said he could see Staffa
away on the right, but Bridie could only see rain—and somehow didn't
mind.

No one minded. They laughed and joked when they got out of the
coach at Fionnphort and battled against the wind and the rain: they
shrieked with counterfeit alarm as they were handed down from the pier
into the tossing, turning, open ferry.

As they left the shelter of the little harbour, a gray wave broke over the bows, splashing everyone who was huddled there.

"All right?" John asked, producing a large white handkerchief and handing it to Bridie to wipe the salt water from her face.

"Quite all right," Bridie answered, delighted to notice that the two girls were looking at her enviously. And at that moment, as the rain streamed down her face as fast as she dried it, she made the most astounding discovery. She was grown-up. And as though that were not enough, she was a completely different person, a girl who exulted in the wind and the rain and the sight of the angry rollers sweeping in from the Atlantic.

In Iona of my heart, Iona of my love,

sang a bearded youth on her other side, his voice only just audible above the noise of the motor and the buffeting of the wind and waves—

Instead of monks' voices shall be the lowing of cattle,
But ere the world shall come to an end
Iona shall be as it was.

"Ere the world shall come to an end," she sang softly to herself. It was an omen. Her world of evasion and imagination had nearly served its purpose. Today, with John to help her, she would close the door into it for ever.

It wouldn't be easy. She'd have to keep him interested in her, like what he liked, admire what he admired, be eager to learn, so that when the right moment came, she could turn to him for the help she knew she needed.

"What was that song someone was singing on the boat?" she asked, as they walked through the village of Iona and then, startled, came to a halt. "It's stopped raining!" she cried. "Imagine. It's stopped raining and I never even noticed!"

"What did I tell you?" John said coolly, thankful that for once the radio forecast had been accurate. "That song? Columba is supposed to have written it: a prophecy of what would happen here. And he was right. Time after time the Vikings plundered and burned the church and slew the monks, until all that was left was a ruin and a handful of crofters with their cattle. It's only quite recently that the Iona Community started the work of restoring the church again."

Raindrops fell like tears from a carved cross: water flooded the cobbled Street of the Dead, along which some sixty kings had been carried to be buried in state in St Oran's Graveyard. With his hand under her elbow, John guided Bridie gently past the sodden grass, the few weathered grey stones—she wasn't ready to face the thought of death again.

As she entered the granite cathedral, turning for a last glimpse of the flock of white doves rising up towards the blue sky, she shivered. It was all so cold and dark. There was nothing to see of Columba's first wooden building, and the Norsemen, time and neglect had destroyed many later ones. But imperceptibly the atmosphere of peace in this new, lovingly restored cathedral took possession of her, and when later she walked by John's side through the cloisters she could feel that here there was comfort and strength.

If Columba had appeared now, she thought, she would have thrown herself on the ground at his feet, sobbing in anguish. She could see the Saint picking her up tenderly and wiping the tears from her eyes. "Tell me your sorrows, child, and I will bring you happiness and surround you with love."

John forgotten, she walked slowly round the precincts with the Saint by her side, and beauty was all around her as the sunlight brought out the soft creams and browns of the granite and sandstone, the green of the slates and the myriad colours in the raindrops which still sparkled on the buildings and in the grass.

Only when they left the Cathedral and set off for the far side of the island did John replace Columba, a John now enhanced—although of course he did not know it—by all the love, understanding and magic that Bridie had attributed to the Saint.

For her, John was now perfect, and Iona was an enchanted island.

They climbed to the top of a hill and ate their lunch, and bemused, she let his talk envelop her, giving every appearance of listening attentively although it was only the occasional sentence or phrase that registered . . . earth goddess . . . Celtic warriors . . . pagans and Christians. Below, white shell-sands edged the little bay and the aquamarine of the sea shaded off into silver on the horizon, where Barra slumbered —Barra, the home of that great-great-grandmother, to whom Bridie owed all the imagination and poetry and love that was hers.

The child really was intelligent, and most discerning, John thought. Of course everyone had done their best for her since Easter, but his parents hadn't the time, his brother and sister the experience, to win her complete confidence. Now was there time to lead her, unobtrusively, to talk of herself and then of her life in London: perhaps by the time they returned to Mull she would have poured out the whole tragedy and he would have achieved his first psychiatric success before he was half-way through medical school.

From his pocket he took out a newspaper cutting. "Have you seen this photograph of your mother, and the crit of her new play?"

The colour drained from Bridie's face.

"I have no mother. That is Jenny Nicholson, the actress. My mother was someone else—old and ugly and screaming at me because I survived the accident when my father was killed." Seizing the paper she tore it across and thrust the pieces back at John.

And when Jenny came to see me in hospital, she thought bitterly, Martin drove her and waited outside. Martin, who'd been in love with her before she even met Daddy. Martin, who'd been poor then but is rich now, and wondering how long he'll have to wait before he can marry her. Ordinary and little and bald. And Daddy so tall and handsome, but not Daddy any more.

"All right, Bridie." John's hand on hers returned her to Iona and the present. "I've got the message. Loud and clear. Now calm down and don't spoil our day."

He'd been a fool, rushing things like that. But it might have worked.

"Tell me how you like living with us in Scotland, Bridie."

*In Iona of my heart, Iona of my love,* Bridie sang silently, dismissing the past and her father with an ease she had never imagined possible; and at the same moment she made the second, quite shattering discovery of the day. Not only was she an adult, but she was in love. Deeply, irrevocably, in love with John.

"Do you need to ask? I didn't know it was possible to be so happy —again."

Had he been older, more experienced, John would have been warned by her fervour, but he was still too concerned with his self-appointed role of mind-healer.

"Would you like to see some more of Iona?"

"I'd rather stay here and talk to you."

Good. To talk of her mother was taboo, but he might get somewhere by introducing the subject of her father. She never tired of talking about him. Now was his chance to see if she was aware when she passed from fact to invention.

"Your father must have had a very exciting life with all the work he did for radio and TV. Which did he prefer?"

"I'd rather you told me about yourself, John. I always wanted a brother, you know. I used to imagine him, devastatingly good-looking and playing rugger for Scot—I mean for England, and all the girls at school would be envious because he looked after me and took me out to dinners and dances and things."

"Most chaps I know take out other chaps' sisters, not their own," John interrupted, concealing his dismay as best he could.

Careful, laddie, he warned himself. She's not content with substituting Mum for her own mother, but now it looks as though she's starting on me. Am I really to be an elder brother? Or . . . ? he gulped.

No, this was neither the place nor the time to attempt to solve Bridie's problems, and perhaps he wasn't the person to try, either.

Hastily he launched into a hotch-potch of stories about Argyll, and when a group of French students approached them for advice on how to see the notorious Corrievreckan whirlpool, he seized the opportunity to prolong the conversation. Bridie, by remaining silent and smiling, gave the impression that she knew as much about the Hebrides as John did: at first she had been furious at the interruption but suddenly she knew she could afford to wait, and that indeed it would be wiser to do so, as now she and John could have other long, blissful days together.

At his suggestion, they collected all the wild flowers they could find and presented them to his mother on their return. Never had she seen Bridie look so relaxed and attractive, Mary thought. Whether or not it was Iona that was responsible for this improvement, she wasn't sure, but she refused to meet trouble half-way.

"Have you noticed how many blues and purples there are now?" she asked, arranging harebells, sea pinks, wild thyme and bell heather, with the dark shiny leaves of bog myrtle, and placing them in an egg-cup. Picking up the yellow St John's wort, she considered where it would look most effective.

"I remember my grandmother saying that her grandmother had told her that if you rubbed your eyes with this flower, you could see the Little People when they were invisible to everyone else," she remarked.

"She didn't say anything about filling up with home-distilled whisky first, did she?" her husband asked.

"Oh, I've no doubt that helped too," Mary agreed. "I expect the Little People were blamed for many a missing sheep or a cow that had been milked before the owner arrived."

"And if anything in the croft was lost or broken, it was fine being able to blame the Little People," Kenneth added. "I wish there were still a few of them around this place."

His father groaned.

"Out with it. What have you bent now?"

"The teapot spout. It wasn't my fault. They shouldn't make them so that they stick out and get knocked against the tap. It's a good thing you didn't like that teapot much, Mum."

"Didn't I?" Mary sounded rather surprised.

"No. I could tell by the way you used to look at it."

"Before long, Mum," John interrupted, "you'll be down on your knees, thanking Little Horror for his kindness in breaking the pot for you."

Bridie joined in the general laughter, though she was only half aware of what was going on around her. She must get John to take her to all the Islands of the Hebrides and especially to Barra. They must visit the slate quarries of Seil and sail to the terrible Corrievreckan. . . .

"When are you leaving us, John?" his mother asked.

"Day after tomorrow."

"Leaving?" Bridie's dreams were shattered. "I thought you had two weeks' vacation." She made no attempt to hide her dismay.

"So I have. But I've arranged with a friend to spend a week walking in the Cairngorms."

"Which friend?" Kenneth asked, mischievously. "The redhead who called here at Christmas in her E-type because she 'just happened to be passing,' or the one who used to write every day and used long yellow envelopes, or the throaty one who was always phoning. . . ." He ducked as his brother aimed a swing at his head. "You've no idea what a harem he has in Edinburgh," he informed Bridie. "And what a harem he had at school."

"I seem to remember someone who nearly howled the school down at the tender age of five," Sheena recalled, "and all because he wasn't allowed to sit by a little girl with red bows in her hair."

"That was different," Kenneth protested. "Her mother kept a general store and gave her a bag of sweeties every morning and afternoon."

Smiling brightly, Bridie got to her feet. She had had a marvellous day, but now she was tired. If they didn't mind, she'd go to her room now and have a lovely, long sleep.

But it was not sleep she wanted. Making no attempt to switch on the light or draw the curtains, she sank into her rocking chair and stared out of the window, heedless of the star-spattered sky, the full moon rising over the mass of Ben More, the Ross road lit up and then plunged into shadow with the passing of the occasional car.

How could they laugh and joke when her one day of perfect happiness had just been destroyed? All desire to return to normal life with its pain and cruelty and searing memories was gone. Why had she ever tried to leave that other world which had never failed to console her, which grew more and more real each time she entered it?

She was in Mexico with her father. And native porters of course. Poisonous snakes and man-eating tigers and saving Daddy's life by split-second shooting. The steamy, impenetrable jungle. The porters disappearing, all except the faithful Pedro, who worshipped her and would have laid down his life for her. Supplies exhausted. Menaced by unseen, hostile tribes.

And then, just as she cried out to Daddy that she could go no farther,

and he, weak though he was, gathered her up in his arms, then she saw it
—the fabulous, lost stone city of the Aztecs, inhabited by a long-
forgotten people. They stared at her in amazement, crowding on to the
city walls, exclaiming that she was their long-awaited princess, and they
came out in a great procession to meet her, singing and dancing and
playing strange musical instruments.

Singing in a strange language.

A woman singing. Harshly. Hypnotically.

Strange musical instruments.

A harp.

With a hoarse croak a raven swooped down on the cottage and landed
on a post in the garden. For a time it perched there, wings folded, tail
tilted, neck and head outstretched as though it could see into the darkness of Bridie's room. Again it croaked, a guttural and menacing sum-
mons which reached through Bridie's world of make-believe so that she
sighed heavily and the rocking chair creaked again as she flexed her
cramped muscles.

# 4 The Washer at the Ford

MEXICO, the stone city, the welcoming procession, her father—all vanished.

The music remained. The plucked notes of a harp and a woman singing in a strange tongue.

When the raven croaked for the third time, Bridie sprang from her chair, put on her red weatherproof coat, walked quietly along the passage and let herself out of the back door. Silent now, the bird launched itself into the air, flying low along the shore of the sea loch and returning in the direction from which it had come.

What time it was, Bridie had no idea. All the lights in the cottage were out, except for one where John was studying behind drawn curtains.

She had no idea where she was going, either.

The raven had destroyed her dream world with its croaking, and now the woman was calling her with her song. She had seen her before, the singer with the harp. Across on the mainland? Yes. The day she and Kenneth had left the others and climbed to the top of the old fortress of Dunadd. Had she always known that wells were the gates to the Otherworld? Had Kenneth known?

(In his bed Kenneth stirred, sat up and looked sleepily out of the window. What on earth was Bridie doing out there at—he glanced at the luminous hands of his watch—nearly midnight? He fumbled for his shoes, pulled on the old school mac which would soon be too small for him, and left the cottage as silently and by the same door as Bridie had done.)

Hearing her name called, Bridie turned and waited for Kenneth to catch her up.

"What's the big idea?" he demanded. "Why choose this time to go for a walk when you've been out all day?"

"I have to go, Kenneth. That woman with the *clarsach* is calling me. Can't you hear her?"

Kenneth listened.

"You're crazy," he said. "Come on back." He reached for her wrist to turn her round, and stiffened. "That's funny," he muttered. "I can hear it now. She was on Dunadd with some other queer characters. How could I possibly forget about that?"

"Are you coming with me, then?"

"You bet!" He was growing excited now. "There was a tall man and a dwarf, and someone lying on a couch, wasn't there?"

"Yes. And we saw them again one afternoon by the lochside, just back there a little. No. It wasn't you I was with. It was Sheena, and Calum."

(Sighing in her sleep, Sheena turned towards the window and opened her eyes. When she first saw the two silhouetted figures hurrying away from the cottage she thought she was dreaming. Even when she fastened her sandals and knotted the cord of her dressing gown around her she thought it was still a dream.

As for Calum, he and a couple of cronies, fortified by a great deal of whisky on which no duty had been paid, had spent the entire day recalling the evictions of the crofters during the previous century, and though he wakened for a moment, it was only to groan and fall asleep again.)

"Sheena saw them too, did she? She never said anything to me about them." Kenneth sounded faintly aggrieved. "I wonder if she told John? Those two often gang up together against me."

(He really was too tired to absorb any more, John thought, closing his books and retracting the point of his ball pen. Yawning, he switched off the light and drew back the curtains in time to witness what appeared to be a puppet shadow drama set against a most improbable background of moonlight, loch and mountain. There was even an impossibly huge black raven perched on a stunted thorn tree. Two of the figures, Bridie and Kenneth, were arguing heatedly with the third, who obviously must be Sheena, although it was hard to tell as she was partially obscured by the others. There was a great deal of gesticulating until Bridie shrugged her shoulders and turned away, whereupon Sheena—yes, it was Sheena —made a grab at her, and then stood absolutely still, head tilted, as though listening intently. Obviously at this point some form of agreement was reached, because they joined hands and hurried off along the road, towards the head of the loch, with the impossible raven leading the way.

"The young idiots," he muttered. "What are they up to? Sheena, of all people!" He hunted for his pullover, let himself out of the front door, and hurried after them.)

At first they walked, Sheena in the middle and Kenneth and Bridie on either side, and then, as the eerie singing and the music grew more demanding, they started to run.

Faster they went and faster. It was all so effortless that Bridie wasn't sure whether or not at times her feet actually left the ground and she was flying.

"I'm dreaming," she said, as they passed a derelict bothy that was still a furnished home in the imagination of a third-generation Australian farmer. "If I wake up, you two will vanish."

"If I wake up, you'll vanish," Kenneth retorted.

Ahead of them the raven croaked triumphantly and swooped down to land on the top of a bleached elder, riven by lightning the previous year. Again it croaked, spreading its wings to their full extent, and then folded them again and sat there, hunched and silent.

At the same time the three came to a halt, and gazed around them in bewilderment.

Bridie saw her first.

She sat on a low boulder by the spit of land which jutted out into the loch, and Bridie remembered her uncle pointing out the place to her on her first day here—where once pilgrims had forded the shallow waters on their journey down the Ross of Mull to Iona. By the woman's side, in an untidy heap, lay swords and daggers, armour and helmets of leather and bronze, decorated shields, tunics, cloaks and the trappings of warhorses and chariot fittings.

"Who is she?" Sheena asked, following the direction of Bridie's gaze. "Why did she make us come here? Bridie, let's go back before it's too late."

Even had she wanted to, Bridie could not have done as Sheena pleaded: the music and singing were magic, irresistible, drawing her forward until she was standing beside the boulder.

It was then that the woman stopped singing, put aside her harp and turned to look at Bridie, pushing back her straggling hair so that the moonlight fell on pale, mocking eyes. A thousand wrinkles creased a face so repulsive that Bridie shuddered as she looked at it, and when the pallid lips drew back in a mirthless smile to reveal shrunken gums and a few blackened teeth, she closed her eyes and turned away.

"Who are you?" she asked in a low voice, trying to control her nausea.

"I am the Washer at the Ford." The voice was winter cold and as grating as the shingle dragged to and fro by the advancing and ebbing waves. "I am as old as the very first word mouthed by Man, and as young as the child born this hour in the cottage in Bunessan.

"Man himself created me from the darkness of his dreams, and the fears that dwell in the half-light before the coming of the dawn: he spun the fabric of my existence from the mists that drift through the corries and over the moorlands and mantle the ruins of ancient forests, and from the spindrift caught by the storm winds as the heavy seas crash on the rocks. Because he feared his fate and yet must know it, he created me, the Hag, who would reveal to him that about himself which he did not know."

"I don't understand," Bridie whispered fearfully.

"Come, my princeling," the Hag commanded, suddenly ignoring Bridie and beckoning to Kenneth. "What will you give me to achieve your heart's desire?"

"Don't go to her, Kenneth," Sheena pleaded. "Stay here with me."

"My heart's desire?" Kenneth cried, breaking free from his sister's hold and running up to the ford. "I don't think there is any one special thing I want just now. I keep on changing my mind, you see."

"Kneel beside me and gaze into the waters of the ford, my adventurous one." Bony fingers plucked the old coat off Kenneth's shoulders. Do not lift your eyes as the waters swirl and move," she ordered, and with a shrill laugh she plunged the coat into the ford. Then, while Kenneth still gazed down, fascinated, she flung the garment on to the heap beside her.

Horrified, Bridie stared at Kenneth's coat. Now a long, jagged tear stretched from shoulder to wrist on the right sleeve; from it there spread a dark stain, and though the moonlight robbed it of its colour, Bridie knew that the stain was red—blood red.

"And the princess who thinks much but says little," the Hag whined, beckoning to Sheena. "Bend your will to the will of the Washer at the Ford, for the ancient gods decreed your fate before you were born. Come to me now, and I will give you your heart's desire."

As she approached the ford, Sheena looked at Bridie as though trying to say something, to plead with her perhaps, or to warn her, and then, sighing, she knelt beside her brother, making no protest when the Hag snatched away her dressing gown, plunging it in the water as Sheena gazed down as though hypnotized. Carelessly the Hag tossed the garment aside, and though it remained whole a dark stain spread over the left side, and the cord was curiously contorted.

"And what will you give for your heart's desire?" the old woman demanded, suddenly pouncing on Bridie and forcing her to her knees by the terrible heap of weapons and armour and garments. "This pretty red coat for the dreams and fantasies you have spun during the long days and nights since you were left alone? Look down, my pretty one. Look down."

But this time, instead of plunging the red coat in the water, the Hag hunted through first one pocket and then the other, and with a triumphant screech brought out a crumpled white handkerchief, which Bridie recognized with mounting fear as the one John had lent her when they crossed in the ferry to Iona.

"Sheena! Kenneth!"

No one moved as John ran along the road and crossed to the old ford.

"Bridie!" He was out of breath and very angry. "What's happening? What are you all doing here, kneeling like this? Sheena, what on earth are you starinng at?"

"You mean you can't see her?" Sheena asked, her voice scarcely more than a whisper. "She's got your handkerchief, one of those I embroidered with your initial for last Christmas"—only Bridie saw the momentary look of fear on the Hag's face, and not till long afterwards did she understand its cause—"and she's going to wash it in the ford. Oh, John, if she offers you your heart's desire, don't tell her; don't even think of it."

"If who offers me my heart's desire? I've no idea what you're talking about, Sheena. Don't you think it's time you stopped playing games and went back to the cottage?"

But Bridie knew from the glitter of the Hag's eyes that for a fleeting second John had thought of something he dearly wanted.

"Can't you see her?" Sheena asked. "She's just beside you. The Washer at the Ford. And now she's dipping the handkerchief in the water!"

Shuddering, Sheena drew away as the Hag lifted out the tattered, blood-soaked rag and let it flutter on to the heap at her side.

"Give him his sight and his hearing," the woman commanded Bridie, and, sickened, she remembered that it was only when she touched them that Kenneth and Sheena had been able to see the Singer, hear the Song.

"I won't!" she cried. "Why don't you leave me alone?" Now she recognized the Hag as a creature from those nightmares which had so terrified her after her father's death, nightmares which were returning just when she thought she was free of them. "I don't know who you are or what you want. I don't want to think about them. They're older than me, and happy. They can look after themselves. I'm alone and I've been ill. Please don't wash my coat in the waters of the ford. Please!"

The Hag laughed shrilly.

"There is no need for me to do that now. You will achieve your heart's desire, but the price will be paid by others."

"Oh, no, no." Bridie began to sob helplessly.

"It's all right, Bridie." Trying to keep his voice calm and reassuring, John turned from his sister. "Don't upset yourself. I won't let anyone harm you. Come along. I'll take you back home—all of you."

He stooped to help Bridie to her feet and froze, drawing in his breath sharply. Now he could see the Hag.

Far away, in a shadowed corrie in the hills, a young stag bellowed an impatient challenge, an assertion of his right to assume power, and before the echoes had died away, was answered scornfully by the leader of the herd, his own sire.

"Who are you?" John asked, his eyes on the Hag.

"Take Sheena away, John," Bridie screamed, ashamed now of her last, selfish outburst. "And Kenneth. Quickly, before it's too late." She turned to the Washer at the Ford. "Leave them alone. Take me with you if you must, but please leave them alone."

"You're coming with me, Bridie," John said steadily, taking her by the hand and helping her to her feet just as a swirling grey mist swept down from Ben More, blotting out the moon and the stars, the loch and the lonely road, the raven hunched on the leafless tree, and the Washer at the Ford.

Bridie felt John's grip tighten as he sought to find and reassure his brother and sister, but their cries were strangely muted, and it seemed as though the mists which surged and boiled around her were now penetrating her head, numbing her brain. Ghostly voices pressed down on her: the savage cries of war-maddened fighters, the hoarse laughter of triumphant marauders, the pitiful moans of the helpless and the unprotected.

Her feet were no longer on the ground.

"Hold tight, Bridie," John shouted. "I'll look after you." And then they were swept up into the mist, higher and still higher, spinning dizzily round and round, with those fearful, agonizing cries pressing on their ears.

What could John do, Bridie thought despairingly, knowing that already she was lost, one with the mists and the voices. Round and round, higher still and higher, bludgeoned by the wind and the cries into some primeval, amorphous being, blind, uncomprehending and mindless.

Slower now. Sinking in silence. Sinking until at last the ground was beneath her feet.

Silence.

She was cold. So cold.

A bitter wind sent ice arrows of hail to seal her eyelids and chill her flesh. A thousand fingers seized her, plucked at her torn clothes, stabbed and pricked, jostled and bumped: a thousand voices whispered and argued, laughed and mocked to the whirr of spinning wheels, the clatter of weaving looms.

So cold.

A cock crowed.

"Bridie! Are you all right? Bridie!"

Slowly, agonizingly, warmth and life seeped through her limbs and body, and just when it seemed this new accompanying pain was more than she could bear, it vanished, and she stretched her arms and opened her eyes.

They were in a wood, in a clearing lit by a dim, green light as hazy sunlight filtered through the tossing leaves. She was sitting on a fallen trunk which glowed with the eerie phosphorescence of decay, while opposite, leaning against a lichen-covered rock, John stared at her in bewilderment.

"Are you all right, Bridie?" he repeated.

"Ye-es. At least, I think so. But what happened? Was it a whirlwind?"

"I don't know. I don't know what happened or where we are. But no whirlwind is responsible for that." He pointed at Bridie, and looking down, she caught her breath, awed and incredulous.

Never before had she possessed a dress anything like this. Nervously at first, and then sensuous pleasure giving her increasing confidence, she stroked the pale green silk gown and traced with an exploratory finger the intricate design of leaping animals, embroidered in gold and silver thread on the breast and shoulders.

She had given herself a colour rinse before she'd left Oban, but surely her hair hadn't been this beautiful pale gold? And had it ever been as long and thick?

Mystified, she looked at John as he sat there in his brown cords and yellow pullover.

"Concussion," he muttered. "That's it. I must keep quite calm. Naturally I'm feeling confused. Now, let me think. You are Bridie. But I can't remember my own name."

"It's John."

"John what? No, don't tell me. It'll come in time. And then the question is: where are we? No, don't tell me that either."

"I wasn't going to, I don't know. I've never been here in my life." Ah, but which life? Bridie wondered. There'd been a different kind of life before the wind had snatched them up, and there had been people other than John in it. She knew it was terribly important that she should never forget the existence of that world, although the reason for remembering it eluded her at the moment.

Meanwhile, there was the question of here and now, of this strange, green-lit clearing, which perhaps she had once known, long ago.

Exhilarated by a peculiar feeling of power, she sprang to her feet. But before she could take the first step away from the clearing, habit and training asserted themselves, and she stood absolutely still, listening —tense at first and then gradually relaxing as the familiar sounds brought reassurance. She identified them all: the rustling of leaves and the creaking of branches, the soft squeaks, mutterings and grunts of the small creatures whose homes were in the undergrowth, the shrill pipings, calls and whistlings of the birds in the tree tops. Partially satisfied, she closed her eyes and sniffed like a wild animal, turning her head this way and that, distinguishing by their characteristic odours the different varieties of trees, the tangled plants of briars, brambles, garlic and ferns, and the woodland animals living there. Yes, all was exactly as it should be.

"Brigid!" So faint. So strange and yet so familiar.

"We must go, John," she cried excitedly. "There's no time to lose. Follow me."

"Bridie, wait! What's the hurry? And where are you going, anyway?"

"Don't ask me now, John. I can't explain. All I know is that I am to lead you along this track."

Holding up her long silk dress with one hand, she set off through the wood, experiencing an inexplicable feeling of nostalgia as she saw or smelt some flower or plant which linked her with that other world they had just left. When the characteristic reek of foxes or wild swine assailed her, she trod carefully, knowing that wary eyes would be watching them although she could see nothing: once she picked up the odour of a mountain cat and its young, but it was stale—at least twenty-four hours old.

As the trees began to thin out and the sun to beat down on them, the track turned into a sheltered pocket half-way up the side of a low hill. Here there were signs of the work of Man: oaks, ashes and elms had been felled, and others, bearing fruit and nuts, planted in their place. Beyond, tall foxgloves waved the last of their mauve flowers at the top of thick stems; the dull purple bells of deadly nightshade drooped among the dying spikes of wolfsbane and the foetid leaves of black hellebore.

"Bridie!" John called out. "Wait a minute. There's something about this place that worries me. I don't think we should go any farther just now."

Bridie swung round to chide him angrily, but seeing his distress and uncertainty, she remembered he was a stranger in her world and immediately felt glad that she was able to reassure him.

"It's quite all right, John. I know where we are now. Just follow me."

"No, Bridie. Wait. I'm no botanist, but all the plants that I can recognize here are poisonous ones. And they've been deliberately cultivated. Suppose some child. . . ."

"No child would ever come here, John. Only those who work for Broichan are allowed on this hill."

"Who on earth is Broichan?"

"You'll meet him soon." The sooner the better, she thought, because she didn't know either. The name was familiar, but the man? Memory was returning, but everything was so disconnected.

Her ears picked up the splash of the burn as it tumbled over rocks and dropped to peaty pools, and she remembered the palisade of rough-hewn timbers the moment she saw it. Confidence returned when she observed that the gates were wide open. Broichan must have been very sure of her return, though there was no sign of him on the verandah of his heather-thatched dwelling, and the House of Secrets beside it was locked as usual.

"I expect he'll be in one of the dormitories among the trees, higher up the hill," she said.

"Who will?" There was more than a hint of irritation in John's query.

"Broichan."

The long grass on which they were now walking was patterned with eyebright and creeping jenny, and the air pleasant with the scent of wild thyme.

"He's in that shelter, John."

"Broichan?"

"Of course not," Bridie answered shortly, angry because she did not know herself. But it was all familiar: the shelter with its three sides of closely interlacing branches, up which climbed honeysuckle and other plants with names she could not recall; the fourth side, its screen removed, was open to the sun.

She recognized the figure on the couch at once, although the woollen rugs which once covered him had slipped to the ground.

I saw him on Dunadd in Argyll, she thought, and on the shores of Loch Scridain on Mull, and although his face was turned away from me, just as it is now, I'm sure I've known him all my life.

"Where are we?" John asked, staring about him and beginning to yield to exasperation.

"In the Place of Healing."

On the couch the young man sighed and turned slowly so that they could see his closed eyes, his face pale and drawn with suffering, the wounds on his neck and legs, and the heavily bandaged left arm.

I must have known what to expect all along, Bridie thought, as she watched John staring at the face of the young man.

"Who is he?" he demanded, one hand stealing up to trace the features of his own face and then slowly rubbing his chin with his knuckles. The familiar gesture brought back the name which had eluded her.

"Aidan, Prince of Dalriada."

"He . . . he reminds me of someone."

Bridie said nothing. In time John would find out for himself.

"What happened?"

"I'm not quite sure. They decided to fight the Northern Picts. They wouldn't listen to me. Aidan must have been wounded in the battle."

"Picts? Dalriada?" John looked at her sharply. "Bridie, what are you talking about? You're making it all up, aren't you? Just as you did about your father and. . . ."

He broke off abruptly. Anger gave way to incredulity and then to horror as he saw the flat head weaving sideways with its flickering tongue, the long green and brown body undulating with incredible swiftness towards them. Out of the corner of his eye he saw another rippling movement among the grass, and another.

The whole place was alive with snakes!

Rigid with fear he waited, not knowing what to do. Beside him a clump of crumpled red poppies swayed and three petals detached themselves and floated idly to the ground as a viper emerged from their tangled stems. Swiftly it slid on to the chest of the wounded prince and, tongue darting in and out, poised its ugly head a few inches above the eyes of the unconscious man.

# 5  The Place of Healing

"OH, NO!" John shouted, his own fear forgotten in the peril to which the wounded man was exposed. Lunging forward, he grabbed the snake under its head and flung it writhing and squirming, as far away from the shelter as he could. Before he could deal with any of the others, however, Bridie seized his arm.

"It's all right," she assured him. "There's nothing to worry about. They're quite harmless. They've all had their poison sacs removed. That one was just going to lick the corner of Aidan's eyes very gently, to keep them clean. We use snakes to clean wounds too. It's been part of our treatment for hundreds of years. Broichan says we first learned it from a Roman legionary our forefathers captured when they attacked the Great Stone Wall, and he said that the Romans had learned it from the Greeks."

"I only hope you're right, and they haven't overlooked one of the blighters," John said, eyeing the snakes uneasily, and then his attention was distracted by the boy now approaching and carrying a clay bowl with great care.

"Kenneth!" he cried.

Startled, the boy looked up, stared first at John and then at the unconscious man, and with a cry of alarm dropped the bowl so that it broke in pieces and the liquid in it spilled at his feet.

"Who is he, daughter of the High One?" he asked, looking to Bridie for help. "Is he some relative of the prince, my foster brother?"

"Kenneth!" John strode forward and grasped the boy's arm. "What are you doing here? Why are you dressed in that ridiculous tunic? Kenneth, don't shrink from me. I'm John—your brother John."

"I do not understand him, daughter of the High One. What is this strange tongue that he speaks?"

"Kenneth!" John shook the boy angrily. "Stop playing this stupid game and answer me properly."

"Kenneth isn't playing a game, John," Bridie interposed quickly. If the boy had existed in that world from which she and John had come, she could remember nothing of him. "Prince Aidan was brought up in Ireland with Kenneth's family. They are foster brothers, and Kenneth

was sent here three months ago as Aidan's personal attendant. He is
speaking Celtic because that is the only language he knows. He's called
Kenneth because that is a Celtic name."

"I don't believe it," John said flatly, but he relaxed his grip on the
boy's shoulders. "I'm dreaming. I'll wake up soon, and at breakfast,
when I tell the family about this, they'll laugh. Kenneth'll laugh loudest
of all."

"Broichan!" Bridie had no time for either John or Kenneth now. The
old happiness and excitement surged through her as she looked past
them to the man who had appeared so quietly on the verandah.

It seemed an eternity since she had seen him, and she would have run
up to him, flung herself in his arms, had she not caught the warning in
his dark, deep-set eyes.

Appearances had to be kept up in front of others, above all on formal
occasions. How impressive he looked, she thought: his cloak of brown
hide was tossed over his linen robe and fastened on the right shoulder
with a splendid brooch of topazes, pearls and opals set in a design of
filigree silver; gold ear-rings glittered against his smooth, tanned cheeks
and his black, waving hair fell to his shoulders beneath the great
ceremonial head-dress of multi-coloured birds' feathers, its wings
fashioned from the flight pinions of hawks, buzzards and golden eagles.

"So Brigid, daughter of the High One, has returned to us, smiling
with attractive innocence, as though nothing had happened," a hoarse
voice cried, and Bridie's elation vanished as Drust the Dwarf sidled out
of the dwelling to stand beside his master, long arms hanging loosely by
his misshapen body, malicious eyes peering from under the tangled mat
of his red hair.

Returned? She picked up the word, toyed with it casually as though it
were of no importance, and of its own accord it awakened the sleeping
memory.

She was standing in the Great Hall, in the fortress of Dunadd, and
for the first time in her life she asserted herself. She flayed them all with
her tongue—Gabran, the king, Broichan, the high priest, Aidan and all
the captains and fighting men—for planning to challenge the forces of
Brude, king of the Northern Picts, when she had proved by her divi-
nations that the time was not propitious, the auguries were all
unfavourable.

Oh, they had paid lip service to her wisdom and magic, thanked her
for her advice—and gone ahead with their arrangements to fight: even
Broichan had suggested that perhaps, in her youth and inexperience,
she had made some vital mistake somewhere. Had she checked the position of the stars and the phase of the moon before picking her plants

and digging her roots? Had she taken into consideration the flight of the birds at the crucial moment, their exact number and direction?

Furious at this casual and amused rejection of what she knew to be a well-founded warning, she had flung out of the Hall and ridden off to the far border of the Great Moss, where no one would think of looking for her. There, in the Place of Green Maidens, a grass-covered knoll surrounded by grey, lichen-patterned stones erected for some unknown purpose by a people long forgotten, there she had flung herself down and wept.

And then? But memory faded.

"You fought?" she said slowly, feeling her way. "In spite of my warning, you fought!"

From the momentary flicker in his dark eyes she knew that Broichan was aware of her uncertainty and at the same time was bargaining with her. Help him now, and all would be as it had been in the past.

"The gods abandoned us," he admitted. "We were outnumbered. Gabran was killed along with seven of our most èxperienced warriors. The prince"—he gestured towards the shelter where Kenneth was bathing the forehead of the restless man—"was so badly wounded that I knew I could not heal him without help."

"I told her," Drust interrupted. "I tracked her down that night to the Place of Green Maidens and told her we needed her Girdle of Healing for the prince, the girdle which you yourself had given her at the Feast of Samuin.

"I should have been wary when she parted with it without a word —that delicate silverwork girdle set with rubies and amethysts—but I thought only of the prince as I hurried back. Not until dawn broke and the false girdle turned to rushes in my hand, did I realize how I had been tricked. When I returned to her hiding place, she had gone."

Yes, Bridie thought. The Green Maidens took pity on me as I lay there weeping. "Give us your magic Girdle of Healing," they said, "so that we can help those who are sick. In its place we will give you a girdle that looks exactly the same, as long as only you wear it. Do this and we will send you far away from Dalriada into the Unborn Years, where you will have to make no decisions, accept no responsibilities."

So it was in the world of the Unborn Years that she had met John, she thought. The memory of her stay there was fading as her life here became more vivid, but she was sure that then she had been a happy, carefree, much-loved girl.

"The girdle was mine," she said coldly. "How was I to know you would ask for it back within a year of your giving it to me?"

Broichan kept silent, but Drust was too angry to follow his example.

"Because you refused to help us, O daughter of the High One, Broichan had to humble himself before the Washer at the Ford, and seek her help. Do you know the agony of mind and body we endured, the prayers we offered and the sacrifices we made so that our souls might leave our bodies on the *clarsach* music of the Hag, to search for a Healer from among the descendants of the prince—one who bore his face and form but had greater knowledge of healing than even Broichan, the high-priest?

"Twice we endured that agony, but in vain, because of your interference, O Brigid. The third time, the magic of Broichan prevailed, but for the third time you interfered, returning with the Healer to a kingdom you had declared you never wanted to see again."

"Hold your tongue, Drust," Bridie cried angrily, "and let me speak with my priest." She watched as the dwarf scowled, spat on the ground and turned away, and then she looked at Broichan. "Have you no word of apology that you rejected my advice and caused my people to pay dearly for this rejection?

"Have you no word of greeting that I have returned to you from the Unborn Years? Since when has Drust the Dwarf become your spokesman?"

"High One . . ."

"Drust says I interfered when you summoned a Healer from the Unborn Years." She steeled herself to resist that slow, easy smile which had always won her over in the past. "Because he did not welcome my return, he asserts that you did not want me either."

"High One . . ."

"There is your Healer." She forced herself to ignore the soft, coaxing voice that had been irresistible until now. "See if your powers will help you to communicate with him, Broichan."

The priest glanced at Drust, but the dwarf now seemed to be lost in his own thoughts, and so, drawing himself up to his full height, he called out; "Listen to me, O Healer from the Unborn Years!" John, who was kneeling by the unconscious man, glanced up briefly and then returned to contemplate, with growing incredulity and concern, the manner in which the wounds had been dressed. "With your great knowledge you must heal our prince now, because he cannot last out the night."

When John paid him no attention, Broichan strode forward, his face scarlet with anger, and jerked him to his feet.

"Hey! Steady on! What do you think you're doing?" John demanded. "I wasn't interfering with your patient. I was only looking at him."

"What does he say?" Broichan asked, turning to Bridie in dismay.

"I suppose this Broichan of yours is speaking in Celtic because it's the only language he knows," John commmented sarcastically. "Will I be glad when I wake up!" He looked thoughful. "How you speak Celtic and English too beats me."

"Yes, but I can," Bridie retorted. This was a weapon she meant to use for her own ends.

"Perhaps you understand now, Broichan, why I accompanied the Healer back here. You would otherwise have had some trouble, I think, in making yourself understood."

"Bridie," John interrupted, "will you stop jabbering away and tell me one thing? Is this chap in fancy dress a doctor?"

"He is our chief priest. I suppose he is a kind of doctor. No, let me finish. Broichan has brought you back through the years for two reasons.

"The first is that you are descended from Aidan and therefore you're closer to him than anyone else.

"The second is that in the fourteen hundred years or so which separate Aidan and you, Broichan thinks you must surely have learned magic and a knowledge of healing greater than his, and so you'll be able to save Aidan's life."

"I don't believe it," John said, but now there was a note of uncertainty in his voice. "Kenneth, can you really not understand what I'm saying?"

The boy, who had returned with another bowl of water and was bathing the prince's forehead, got to his feet. Slowly he passed his hand over John's face and then he pointed to the wounded man.

"I am only his foster brother," he said, "but I would die for him. You are his real brother. You must save his life because only you have the knowledge."

"All right, Bridie. Don't translate. I can guess. But what I'd like to know is, just who is having who on?"

Bridie stamped her foot angrily.

"Whether you believe me or not, you stubborn idiot, can't you see that Aidan is dying? Isn't there anything you can do to save him? Broichan has done all he can."

"I'll say he has," John agreed, making no attempt to hide his feelings as he looked down at the mess of clotted blood, moss and cobwebs on the injured man's body.

Watching Broichan's face darken, and knowing how he resented criticism of any kind, Bridie stepped forward hastily.

"Tell the Healer of the great magic you have already used to help the prince," she begged. "When I have translated all, then he will understand how truly great you are." Appeased by the flattery, Broichan nodded his head.

"The Healer must understand that from the very first I encountered such difficulties as I had never known before. Although the gods listened to me, they answered neither yes nor no when I asked that the life of our prince should be spared, so that I did not know whether or not they had deserted me, as you had done, O daughter of the High One.

"Nevertheless, I persevered. I chanted the one hundred and one praises of the High One, your mother, and the seventy-seven binding spells of the Great White One and the three and thirty supplications to the Unknown Gods.

"I bathed the prince in healing water collected the first moment the rays of the sun had quickened it, and I staunched the wounds with moss soaked in wine and vinegar, and in cobwebs fortified with the white of eggs and the juice of nasturtium seeds.

"I applied leeches to suck the poison from the spear wound in the thigh and then drew together the gaping edges with linen thread."

"Did he mention anything about sterilization?" John demanded, when all this was conveyed to him.

"That is not a word we Celts know."

"I can't think how you Celts survive at all—the men, anyway."

"Generally they don't," Bridie agreed. "But it doesn't matter. We believe it's good to die in battle. Our men know they'll be born again, many times, to fight even more valiantly."

"Have you asked him what he can do to save the prince?" Broichan demanded testily.

"Look, Bridie. Explain to him that I'm not a qualified doctor. I'm only half-way through my training, and I'd be kicked out of medical school if I tried to practise. And even if I were fully qualified, there's absolutely nothing I can do here—I've no drugs, equipment, not even a thermometer, though that's the last thing I need to tell me that chap's temperature is way above normal."

"Bring him to the House of Secrets. There he may avail himself of such of my remedies as he wishes," Broichan ordered.

"You're greatly honoured," Bridie whispered. "No one is ever allowed in the House of Secrets except the high priest. Not even me." She shivered.

"Frightened?"

"Of course not. I'm the daughter of a goddess, and far more powerful than any priest."

"Good heavens! You're cr. . . ."

He'd been going to say she was crazy, Bridie thought, but he wasn't so sure now. Poor John!

Inside the House of Secrets, however, his face was inscrutable as they surveyed the rows of containers: boxes made from birch and lime, oak and elm, tin, copper and finely engraved silver; phials of opaque green glass, tall and slender-necked or curved and squat; vessels of multi-coloured horn stoppered with clay, and earthenware pots and bowls of all shapes and sizes.

"This chap could make a fortune in the herbal remedy line," he said at length, when all the contents and their uses had been described to him. "Does he realize that he's got enough poison among this little lot to wipe out all the inhabitants of Oban and still have plenty left over?"

"Of course he knows that. But no one has ever died in Dalriada unless the gods called them."

"And that's a fine let-out, I must say." He shook his head as they walked out into the open air again. "I don't know what to say, Bridie. By rights, that chap across there should have died of blood poisoning. Those wounds should all be infected, but they're not. They're heal-ing—the ones I can see, anyway."

"You mean Aidan will live?"

"No. He'll die, I'm afraid. But not of his wounds. Of loss of blood."

Broichan could contain himself no longer.

"Daughter of the High One, I have offered the Healer all the know-ledge and wisdom won over thousands of years by our priests and healers. Tell him that, if with this and his own learning, he does not immediately save the life of the prince, I will order Drust to strangle him, and I myself will place his head over the gateway of Dunadd!"

"In that case, you might have spared yourself the trouble of bringing him here through the years, O Broichan. What will you achieve by kill-ing him? Give me a little time to convince him that his powers are greater than he knows."

She turned to John, but he had left them and was now on his knees by Aidan's side, watching as the prince opened his eyes and the ghost of a smile touched his lips.

"Broichan said that he could reach out through the years to bring you back—you, who are the future me, so that you could help me, who am the past you. It is not for myself that I need help, but for my people, who are now your people. You must heal my wounds, for I have waited long, and I am weaker than I was on the day I was born."

Bewildered, John stared into eyes the same blue as his own. "Why can I understand every word you say when I don't know your language or understand when anyone else speaks it?"

"That is because we are brothers. I too can understand you. But

—my wounds?"

"The ones I can see are healing. Do you want me to look at your arm?"

"Of course. I shall be interested to see it myself. It is a wound I received after I had fallen, unconscious, from my chariot."

As John began to unwind the bandage, Broichan drew Kenneth and Bridie to one side.

"This will cause the prince great pain and will need to be bandaged again immediately," he said in a low voice. "Kenneth, go to the main dormitory in the woods and ask Riannon, who is in charge of supplies, to give you clean linen bandages and thread. And bring a bowl of fresh water from the stream.

"And you, Brigid, daughter of the High One, return to the House of Secrets and find the blue phial with the silver stopper which stands by itself on the highest shelf. Take it to Odras in the kitchen. Tell her to cease whatever she is doing and prepare a draught for deep sleep. Then bring it to me here yourself. Hurry."

When at length Bridie returned, the hand was bandaged and the sweat was standing out on Aidan's forehead.

"Odras was not in the kitchen," she said, to avert Broichan's anger at her delay. "In the end I found her in the slaughter-house, cutting up a newly killed sheep." And she handed over the draught in the beaker.

"Bridie, come here!" John called out, and drawing her to one side, he lowered his voice. "Now, answer me honestly. Have we really gone back in time somehow, to the Dark Ages? Is this really Celtic Scotland, the kingdom of Dalriada?"

"Yes, John. It is." She returned his gaze without flinching, wondering why he was finding it so difficult to accept what had happened.

"And no one has any idea what a blood transfusion is?"

"No."

"Then there's nothing I can do. Nothing." Dejected and ashamed, he turned away, unable to meet her plea for help.

"John, how did they do them—blood transfusions—at the very beginning, when they had to invent their own equipment?"

When he made no answer, she closed her eyes. Although she knew there was some reason why she must not forget her life in the Unborn Years, she was aware that its memory was growing more faded and blurred as she was caught up in the world around her. She forced herself to concentrate. This girl looking at a book, a history of medicine, and the engraving which had aroused her indignation: a lady dying from loss of blood after childbirth, and the coachman volunteering to give her his blood. The coachman, not the husband!

John stared at her.

"Goddess or girl, you're right, Bridie."

Bridie smiled. He didn't realize that she hadn't spoken, that he had read her thoughts.

"But the risks, Bridie. The appalling risks."

"The Healer must have blood. A great deal of blood," Bridie said, turning to the Priest.

For a moment Broichan looked startled, and then he nodded.

"The Great White One demands the lives and the blood of men frequently, so why should not a prince?" he agreed.

"No one is to be killed for me," Aidan said, trying to sit up and exert his authority, but finding all movement beyond him. "I have drunk all the foul-tasting draughts you have given me, Broichan," he continued weakly, "but I will not drink the blood of a man."

"You don't drink it," John reassured him.

"Then how. . . .?"

"Through your artery." John demonstrated on his own arm.

"But whose blood?" Broichan asked softly.

"Mine!" Kenneth cried, drawing his dagger and placing it at his throat.

"We shall need you to care for him afterwards," John said, removing the dagger and patting the boy on the head. "Not just any blood. It must be the same group as his. But I don't know his group. And couldn't match it if I did."

Aidan looked at him.

"We are one, you and I, John. My people are your people. My enemies are your enemies. Our minds are the same. And our bodies."

"Our blood?"

"Of necessity, it must be the same too. Is it important?"

"Very. But you give me confidence."

"The prince will need a sleeping draught afterwards," Broichan said smoothly. "I have it ready in this beaker. It is from the root of the plant nightshade, dried, boiled in wine and strained. It will give at least three to four hours' sleep. Do not be alarmed. Be assured that I know its powers to cure, and to kill."

"Mind reader?" John muttered to Bridie. "Or shrewd guesser? Keep quiet. Let me think." No one spoke. "For goodness sake stop staring at me as though I'm a ruddy miracle worker!" he shouted.

"They want to help," Bridie pointed out. "Give them something to do."

"Right. Tell Kenneth to get a large leaf and use it to keep the flies and mosquitoes away from Aidan.

"Next. Apparatus. What did they use in those early days? Tubes of silver and rubber and glass syringes. Hopeless. Tubes—something hollow, firm and clean."

"Reeds?" Bridie suggested.

"That's it. Any near here? Good. Tell that scowling redhead to go and cut me several healthy plants. I want half a dozen pieces about this length"—he measured the size with his hands—"hollowed out and every bit of pith removed. Then tell him to wash them in the stream, again and again and again. You'd better give them a final rinse," he added. "I don't care much for the colour of his hands."

"Now, something pliable to join the two reeds. Bridie, did I hear you say something about a newly killed sheep?"

"Yes. Odras was cutting one up in the slaughter-house."

"I want the ileum. The intestines, girl. Hurry."

Suspicion and distrust darkened Broichan's face when Bridie returned carrying a bowl piled high with unwashed sheep's intestines.

"Tell the Healer that when the prince was first brought here to me, I had killed a sucking pig, and I read the future in both its entrails and its liver. His business is to heal, not to interfere with my skills of divination."

"Pity he didn't divine what a mess he was getting himself into," John commented. "No, don't tell him that. Just say I've no wish to look into the future. And why on earth did you bring the whole lot? All I want is a few inches of gut and a bit of peace so that I can work things out."

Kneeling down again, he smiled at the prince.

"Do you trust me, Aidan?"

"As I do myself, John."

"Good. Then relax and sleep, and when you wake we'll be closer than ever. We'll be blood brothers."

He busied himself with the slippery intestines, using Kenneth's knife to cut off two pieces he hoped would be the right length.

"Wash them," he said to Bridie. "Wash your hands in the running water. Wash the bowl. Then the gut. And the reeds. Put the gut and the reeds in fresh water in the bowl."

"I don't think you need worry so much about hygiene and sterilizing things, John. Aidan's been used to dirt and disease all his life. I should think he's developed a natural immunity by now. "

"Quite. But have I?"

"Oh!" Bridie was taken aback. "I never thought of you."

"Then please don't start now," he said drily. "Fortunately I have a remarkable instinct for self-preservation. Now go and do as you're told. And add some linen thread too."

While Bridie was away, he signalled to Drust and Broichan to help him to pile rugs on the grass and then lift the now sleeping prince carefully on to them: because his arm had to be higher than Aidan's, he arranged a place for himself on the couch and Drust was sent for rugs and animal furs to form a back rest. Finally he set off for the stream himself and washed his hands over and over again.

"Bridie!" he yelled, and when she came running he pointed to the burn. "Scrub up. Immune or not, Aidan's having the highest standards I can rise to. By the way, what about the other patients? And the staff? Where are they?"

"In the dormitories higher up the hill. Broichan has forbidden them to come here because the prince is so ill."

"Good. A goggling audience is the last thing I want. Now, can you help me, Bridie, or are you one of those idiots who faint at the sight of a drop of blood?"

"If you knew the blood that has been shed in the past for my mother, the High One, you wouldn't ask that." Surely the girl of the Unborn Years would never have given such an answer?

"Shall we leave your mother out of it just now and concentrate on Aidan? Now listen carefully. I'm going to explain to you exactly what I hope to do, what I hope to achieve, what might go wrong, and what must be done to put it right.

"At first I shall be able to do most of it myself and I want you to watch, so that if I'm weak or tired later you can take over."

"This is our apparatus." Taking a length of reed he pushed it into the end of a piece of gut and bound it with linen thread, and then a second reed was bound to the other end of the gut. "That's all," he said. "One reed goes in my arm, the other in Aidan's and my blood flows down to him."

He then went on to explain how he would lift and ligature the artery, what he would do if the blood clotted and stopped flowing, and how to close the arteries when the transfusion was completed.

When he had finished, he made her repeat it all after him, and then, with a steady hand and an assurance that he did not feel, he picked up Kenneth's dagger.

He knew he'd have trouble finding Aidan's artery after all the blood the prince had lost but he refused to panic. An eternity later his own blood started to flow down through reed and gut and reed, into the arm of Aidan, Prince of Dalriada.

With a sigh of relief John eased himself against an ill-cured wolfskin rug and prepared to relax. At the same time Broichan stepped backwards from the shelter, threw back his head, and without any warning began to chant in a high, strange voice, quite unlike his own deep one.

"He is singing the Warriors' Low Strain," Bridie whispered, seeing the alarm and anger on John's face. "It's the oldest and most powerful of all our spells. It puts the warrior into an enchanted sleep so that the magic healing can begin. I don't expect you to believe me," she added hastily, "but we think this magic healing is far more powerful than anything that plants and herbs can do."

"What a ghastly racket," John muttered. "Oh, well, I suppose if it keeps him happy, I'll just have to put up with it." He allowed Bridie to bring another rug to put behind his back. "Get another of these contraptions ready, in case the blood clots and we have to switch."

The first time the blood stopped flowing he had to remind her to swab with milk before inserting the second makeshift apparatus.

The second time she had everything ready and performed the changeover without a hitch.

"Good girl," he muttered. "But I wish someone would strangle that man and his Warriors' whatever it is."

"See how the magic of our gods asserts itself!" Broichan exulted, breaking off as John, ashen-faced, swayed sideways and was caught in Drust's long arms. "The Healer and the prince are now one. If the prince lives, so will the Healer: if the prince dies, then the Healer dies with him."

"Tell him to shut up, Bridie. No one's going to die." John was struggling to remain in a world which he knew was fast escaping from him. "You know . . . what to do . . . Bridie?"

"Yes, John. You showed me. I know."

"Wouldn't mind—nice cup of tea," he said, a little later, as he watched Aidan swallow the last of Broichan's sleeping draught.

"Sorry. No tea. Try this." She took the horn vessel that Broichan had just refilled and held it to his bloodless lips. Within a few minutes he was asleep, stretched out on the rug beside Aidan, and now there were only the clothes, and Aidan's battle wounds, by which she could distinguish between the two haggard young men.

"Watch over them carefully, Kenneth," she said, as the boy spread woollen rugs over them. "Sleep by their side, and have one of the slaves to keep you company and help you look after them."

"I shall not sleep," Kenneth answered fiercely. "And I need no slave to keep me company. But my foster-brother will live, O daughter of the High One?"

"Thanks to the Healer from the Unborn Years, he will live."

"I too prayed to my God. Was it your gods or mine who listened and answered?"

Kenneth spoke so softly that Bridie wasn't sure she'd heard him correctly, and she turned away, yawning.

She was desperately tired: all her strength and nervous energy had gone in helping John and giving him confidence. But before she could rest, she must settle matters once and for all with Broichan.

"You are exhausted, poor child," a deep, quiet voice said, and Bridie sighed and allowed Broichan to guide her towards his dwelling. "Come and eat, and then Drust will take you back to your island home in the Loch of the Rowan Tree."

"I will eat, Broichan, after we have talked."

"Is not tomorrow time enough for talking?"

"No."

"Very well, child. Then talk, though I too am weary and exhausted."

No, she would make no response to this all too familiar bid for her sympathy.

"Or perhaps you would rather that I talked? Very well, then." He did not give her time to make any answer. "I was wrong not to listen when you advised against fighting the Northern Picts. I was wrong to neglect you, so that you fled to the Green Maidens for sympathy. I was wrong to try to bring back the Healer without your help."

"Oh, Broichan!"

Never had she expected such an admission from the proud high priest She could hardly bear the sadness and contrition on his face.

"Wait. I have not finished." His voice caressed her, so soft and gentle was it. "All that is bad enough, but my greatest mistake was that I had not noticed the passing of the years. I was blind. I did not see that the child, Brigid, had grown into a beautiful young woman."

He paused, one foot on the step of the verandah and looked down at her perplexedly.

"Perhaps I am not entirely to blame. To me that moment has always been so vivid when we raided the lands of the Northern Picts and I saw the burning homestead, heard the pitiful crying of a baby, and rode in to rescue it—"

"—to rescue me!"

"You, Brigid, just before the burning thatch collapsed. When I returned here to Dalriada, I offered you as a daughter to the High One, and she accepted you. Since that day I have been your high priest as well as hers, teaching you my lore and magic, forgetting that the day would come when you would no longer need me."

"No, Broichan. I shall always need you. You know that."

"Do I, child? I wish I could be as sure of your need for me, as I am of mine for you. But let us forget the past, and rest and eat and talk ogether."

"Not yet. There is one other matter that troubles me, Broichan."

"Yes, child?"

"I think that now I am old enough to meet my mother, the High One. Oh, I know you have told me so often how many people worship her, how many men and women she has to care for, but I am her daughter. You yourself said she accepted me. I have the right to meet my own mother."

"You shall meet her very soon, child," Broichan said with a heavy sigh. "I shall consult the stars and cast spells to find the time most propitious for mother and daughter to meet."

Stroking Bridie's hair gently, Broichan led her inside, and Drust smiled his twisted smile as he hurried forward with the meal he had prepared for them.

# 6    Ceremony at Dunadd

BRIGID AWOKE to the moan of the rising wind, the patter of scudding
sheets of rain on the thatched roof.

Her head ached.

When she tried to sit up she felt so weak it was as though someone
had borrowed her body while she slept and utterly exhausted it. That
such things could happen to others, she knew only too well. But to her?
Never. No enemy, no creature from the Other-world dare offend her
mother, the High One, and Broichan, her priest.

Broichan. Smiling, she closed her eyes again, feeling new strength
stealing through her limbs as she recalled the previous evening and the
meal they had shared. For the first time he had seen her in a new light
—adult, wise and beautiful; he had explained to her all she had meant
to him during the lonely years of her childhood, how he needed her
more than ever.

Dismissing Drust, he explained how important to him were her trust
and support in preventing some of her people from abandoning the old
traditions and customs—even the gods themselves—in favour of new
ideas and a new God who had already found favour with their enemies,
the Northern Picts.

She would support him in every decision he made, she declared, and
there was no further mention of that one occasion when she had
opposed him, and had been right. He had apologized, and the matter
was now to be forgotten. That was as it should be.

Well satisfied and feeling considerably stronger now, she decided it
was time to rise.

"Danu!" she called out.

There was no answer.

"Danu!"

Propping herself on one elbow, she threw aside the covering of brown
bearskins and looked about her.

The fire in the centre of the dwelling was dead and had been for some
time, as only the faintest smell of wood smoke lingered in the air. The
iron cauldron hung from its tripod, but when at last she summoned up
enough energy to leave her couch and cross over to it, it was cold to the

touch, its contents congealed and thickly covered with grease.

Where had Danu gone? She had no right to abandon her mistress like this. She would be soundly whipped when she returned.

Pleasure and satisfaction vanished as she brooded over this inexplicable neglect.

"Danu!" she shouted angrily, and when there was still no answer prowled about the room, swearing that the slave would pay dearly when at last she returned.

In one earthenware bowl she found some cold boiled pork, in another, a gruel made of wheat, barley and honey. Scooping out handfuls, she devoured the contents until both dishes were empty. After a long draught of goat's milk, she flung a rug round her shoulders and went out on to the verandah. Protected by the overhang of the thatched roof, she watched the rain pitting the ruffled surface of the loch which surrounded her dwelling, listening as the blustering wind pounded on creaking trees in the western hills.

Lost in her thoughts, she stood there, motionless, until the angry quarrelling of the ducks in the reeds roused her, and she saw that the rain had ceased. The wind too had dropped a little, but she knew it was resting only to gather its strength: already she could smell the tang of salt water, hear the muted but unmistakable roar of the whirlpools which seethed and boiled between two of the offshore islands.

"Danu!"

Still no reply.

Shrugging her shoulders, she poured some water from the bronze bucket at the door into a clay bowl and washed herself carefully. She tugged at her hair with a bone comb, inflicting a degree of pain she certainly would never have tolerated from her slave, and fastened it behind her ears with two round gold clasps. Picking up the mirror of burnished bronze which Broichan had given her at the Spring Festival of Beltain, she contemplated her face with satisfaction. Broichan was right. She was beautiful. Beautiful and the daughter of a goddess—what more could anyone want?

Turning the mirror over, she let her fingers trace the pattern of loops and swirls and circles so delicately engraved against the background of fine hatchings. She loved her mirror because its craftsmanship never failed to satisfy her need for beauty, and because it was Broichan who had given it to her. Reluctantly she put it down.

Her dress? She should have thought of that first. Danu would be well beaten for leaving her alone like this. It appeared, however, that the slave had remembered that the green dress embroidered with fantastic, prancing creatures was her mistress's favourite, and some time during the night must have washed it, for the stains made by grass and bog had all been removed.

Now the bangle of shale and bronze, the necklace of alternating jet and amber beads, and the latest gift from her people—her coiled-bronze snake ring, the head set with eyes of green glass.

All she needed was her green hooded cloak of finest wool, which she fastened with a gilded bronze brooch and she was ready. But for what?

She knew now that this extreme care in dressing had been merely something to do to ward off the fear she had felt from the moment she awoke, that something was wrong. Something more serious than Danu's absence, though that was bad enough. Whatever it was, she thought, she was going to find out now. She ran round the verandah and over the wooden causeway raised on high stilts above the level of the water but the moment she set foot on the shore, she halted abruptly.

There was no sign of the pony which Drust had tethered to the rowan tree when he accompanied her home the previous evening. As for the rowan tree itself, the guardian of the loch and of her dwelling, it had been uprooted, its branches and leaves torn, its berries crushed, its maimed roots exposed, twisted and naked among the reeds.

The wind? But her tree had withstood gales far worse than this morning's. A band of marauders from the north? Impossible. Armed men from the outposts would have dealt with them long before they got as far as this.

Why pretend when the answer was written in the cloven footprints of the churned earth, the vicious tusk marks on the slender trunk, when even the strong west wind had failed to blow away the characteristic stench?

She shivered. This was the work of the wild swine, and when she told Broichan, he would see that they paid dearly for the insult, no matter how great the god that protected them.

"Danu!" she shouted, but now she neither expected nor received an answer. For a moment she wondered if the beasts had attacked, even killed, the girl, and then she dismissed the thought. Slaves were trained to take care of themselves.

Lifting her skirts, she hurried through the wet heather and bracken and began to climb the winding path which led up through the nearby wood: so concerned was she with premonitions of trouble that she paid no attention to the raindrops which fell from the leaves on to her hair and face and she made no attempt to protect herself by pulling up her hood.

When at last she approached the Place of Healing, her heart sank. The gates in the stockade were closed and from inside came the snarling and baying of the hunting dogs which Broichan left to guard the place in his absence, and she knew that, curled up on the verandah of the House of Secrets, their poison sacs intact, would be two vipers: if an intruder penetrated so far, he would go no farther—and live very little longer.

Ignoring the increasing fury of the dogs, she peered through a gap in the fencing. The shelter where the prince had lain was empty. There was no sound from the offices and dormitories in the wood. What had happened to the wounded warriors who had been there the previous day, to the slaves and staff who had tended them?

"Broichan!" she cried. "Drust! Aidan! Danu!"

The frenzied baying of the hounds was her only answer.

Had some terrible disaster struck during the night while she slept, she asked herself as she left the stockade. She scrambled up through the wood and, without pausing for breath, climbed onto the great rock which crowned the hill top, and stood there, on the strangely carved spirals, rings and cup marks—the work of the giants of the Other-world who had lived here at the beginning of time, long before Rome had sent her armies to build two great walls in the land to the south of Dalriada, before even her people had left their first home in the far east. This rock, Broichan said, had been a lookout post for those long-dead giants, just as it was for her people now.

Although she could not see them all, she knew the exact location of every outpost which guarded the overland trade routes to the north and east and the sea routes of the west. Because she knew where to look, she could pin-point the position of each loch-dwelling, each stockaded farm.

The unease within her mounted.

No one was working in the fields; there were no sheep or cattle grazing in the lush water-meadows, no domesticated pigs were rooting among the trees at the edges of the woods.

What had happened during the night?

The Fort of the Strangers was the nearest outpost, she thought, jumping down from the rock and plunging again into the forest. Like all other outposts, it was manned day and night: unless the garrison had been wiped out by a surprise attack, she would soon know what had been going on in her kingdom.

The track she took was little known: she picked up the rustle of voles and mice, the tiny sigh in the undergrowth as a snake or toad moved out of her way; wild cats, deer, wolves and a bear had crossed the track at different times during the previous night. There was no trace at all of any human being until she came within hailing distance of the Fort of the Strangers, the home of Congus the Cunning, a warrior on whom

Broichan relied greatly. Bridie disliked everything about him: his little pig's eyes, his porcine snout and his smooth, lying tongue which turned every occasion to his own advantage.

From the outpost came the lowing of cattle, the cackling of geese and the squawking of hens. No dogs barked. That meant that already her presence outside was known. Why had the sentry not hailed her in the customary manner?

"This is Brigid, daughter of the High One," she cried in a clear, steady voice. "Why has Congus the Cunning not thrown open his gates in welcome?"

At first she thought there was to be no answer, and then a high-pitched voice replied from the walk behind the palisade, although the speaker himself remained invisible.

"This is Congus, son of Congus the Cunning, O daughter of the High One. My father has been summoned to the Great Hall of Dunadd, to witness the crowning of Aidan as king of Dalriada."

Bridie stared at the solid stone walls topped by their stout wooden palisade and at the massive, firmly shut gates.

"How can the prince be crowned today, when yesterday he was so weak from his battle wounds that he nearly died?" she demanded. "You are mad as well as stupid, Congus, son of Congus. Open the gates at once. How dare you keep the daughter of a goddess standing outside like some slave or beggar?"

"My father said. . . ."

"Open the gates," Bridie ordered, between clenched teeth, "or I swear that, at the next Feast of Samuin, I personally will offer you, alive and screaming, as a meal for the Great White One!"

"What shall I do?" the voice wailed, each word higher and shriller than the last. "My father said he would impale me on the end of his spear, Valiant, if I opened the gates to any man, and you, O daughter of the High One, say you will offer me to the Great White One if I do not."

"Where is your difficulty, Congus, son of Congus?" Bridie asked, changing her tone to one of patient wheedling. "You are not about to open the gates to a man at all, but to the daughter of a goddess."

With what patience she could muster, she waited for the argument to penetrate the thick skull, and then smiled triumphantly as the slaves tugged open the gates, to reveal Congus, son of Congus, his narrow, spotty face almost lost beneath his bronze helmet, his bony legs trembling as he fell on his knees, his eyes fixed, terrified, on the track behind her, in case his father should reappear and set about him before he could explain everything.

"Now, what is all this nonsense about the prince being crowned at

Dunadd today?" Bridie asked, gesturing to the youth to rise but still remaining where she was, so that he had to advance well outside the fortress gates. She halted him before he was too near her.

Her people varied greatly in their attitude to both public and private cleanliness. Congus's fort stank, just as did Congus himself and all his family. A whole day's hunting in the rain made no difference to the smell from both his body and his clothes. If the youth in front of her had not looked like his father, Bridie would have known him immediately from his smell.

"I speak only the truth, O daughter of the High One," young Congus pleaded. "Many indeed thought that Prince Aidan would die of his wounds after the battle with the Northern Picts, when our king, Gabran, was slain. But after you visited the Place of Healing and failed to heal the prince, Broichan, the high priest, called on the Great White One for help; and for three days and three nights he remained with the prince, invoking his most powerful magic and the Great White One listened to Broichan, and spared our prince. Although Aidan has not recovered his full strength, Broichan says he is strong enough to be crowned."

Bridie stared at the stammering youth.

"The prince was ill for three days and nights after I visited the Place of Healing?"

"The goddess has herself been ill," the youth cried nervously. "That same night that she tried in vain to heal the prince, the Marsh People cast a spell on her so that at one moment she was as hot as fire, and then as cold as ice. She knew no one, not Broichan, the high priest, or Drust the Dwarf, or Danu, her slave. Had it not been for the spells of Broichan, the Marsh People would have stolen her life spirit and left only an empty shell. Broichan warned us that there would be no memory of those lost days."

"Three days and nights?" It was Bridie's voice which was shrill now. "I do not believe it!"

"Five days and nights," the youth pleaded, wringing his hands and expecting at any moment to be turned into a bat or slow-worm by the wrathful goddess. "For three days the prince was ill, and for another two he rested and regained his strength. All that time the goddess was in the power of the Marsh People. Broichan said it would be many days before she recovered. He said she might not recover at all, and as he said it, he wept."

Bridie clenched her fists and then let them fall helplessly to her sides. She knew what happened to those who fell victim to the spells of the Marsh People, and she knew also that to recover within five days was most unusual. True, she had felt weak and sick when she wakened this morning. And hungry. And she could not remember anything after her long and confidential talk over supper with Broichan, when he told her how dear she was to him and how much he needed her.

Poor Broichan! How distraught he must have been when Danu sent for him and he realized how ill she was: if only she could have spared him that when he was already fighting for Aidan's life.

"The Healer from the Unborn Years!" she cried suddenly. "He gave his blood to save the prince. What happened to him?"

Young Congus retreated a couple of steps. Was he to become a horse-fly or a sheep tick?

"Alas! When the Marsh People stole the memory of the goddess, they left ghosts in exchange. I have never heard of any such healer, but Broichan can answer questions better than I can."

"Where is Broichan?"

"I have already explained to the goddess. He accompanied the prince to Dunadd early this morning. The ceremony is to be this afternoon. Everyone from Dalriada will be there and will join in the feasting and celebrations afterwards, except those of us who must man the outposts," he added mournfully.

The prince to be crowned king and she, Brigid, daughter of the High One, not there? No matter how ill she had been, someone should have been sent to see if she had recovered sufficiently to attend such a . . . No! No ceremony should have been arranged while she was ill. Who could have persuaded Broichan that she was either too weak or of too little importance to consult?

Furious, she swung round without a word of farewell and set off for Dunadd.

"Shall I signal your approach so that the scouts and guards will recognize you, O goddess?" Congus called after her anxiously.

"May my mother, the High One, wreak her terrible vengeance on any man who does not recognize me without first being told of my approach," Bridie flung over her shoulder, and she kicked at a huge puffball growing from a dead tree trunk, only to have it explode in her face with a vile smell of dirt and decay.

What a fool she was to turn down young Congus's offer, she thought: and she was an even bigger fool not to have borrowed a pony, for already she felt tired and weak, but pride forbade her to return and say she had changed her mind.

She walked on briskly, and where the path divided, she took the right-hand track which entered the forest, shivering in spite of herself as the trees closed in, tossing and groaning in the rising wind. Of late some of the younger warriors had grown over-confident and reckless, attacking with their spears and slings anything that moved in the area they patrolled and asking questions afterwards. She knew that until she reached the flat waste of the Great Moss she would be under surveillance most of the time and so she walked warily.

Twice she caught the characteristic smell of the sweat of a fighting man: when this happened a third time, she called out scornfully to the scout to go back to his mother and learn the difference between upwind and downwind when out tracking.

At length the trees began to thin out and the ground to grow soft and black and yielding until at last it lay before her, the Moine Mhor—the Great Moss, a vast stretch of treacherous, glistening bog.

The wind ruffled the surface of hundreds of evil-looking black pools separated by clumps of emerald moss and uneven stretches of turf; it bent the yellowing leaves of water flags and carried away the sickly sweetness of the orange-spiked asphodel to mingle with the general smell of decaying vegetation. Pale moths fluttered above misshapen objects protruding from the bog: the bleached, white roots of ancient trees or the bones of some unwary beast caught in the yielding moss, sucked down and then spewed up again in the bog's own good time.

Across the Great Moss, winding and twisting like a serpent, fringed with giant rushes far taller than any man, with osiers and broad-leaved water plants, meandered the river, the highway to the ocean.

She drew in a deep breath. A monstrous toad, abandoning for a time the slug it was devouring, stared at her with incurious bronze eyes, and then returned to its meal. It was foolish of her to fear the Great Moss in the daylight, she knew, but that perpetual odour which hung over it, that smell of decay and danger and death, never failed to frighten her.

Picking up a stone, she threw it defiantly into the nearest pool and watched as the thick slime closed over it, sucking it down with a sickening lapping and gurgling, and she remembered the white skull which had leered at her the last time she crossed—a skull which was not that of a beast.

Broichan always laughed at her fears. The Great Moss, he said, protected Dunadd better than all their forts and warriors, and needed neither sleep nor food. And of course Broichan was right. The Great Moss was her friend. It would never harm her. Only in the darkness need she fear it, and its people.

The Marsh People. Five nights ago they had cast a spell on her as she rode back to her home from the Place of Healing. Drust had been with her. Why had he not protected her? She knew the dwarf hated her. She had not realized he was prepared to hand her over to the pitiless Marsh

People and persuade Broichan to crown Aidan while he thought she was still sick.

This time he had gone too far. This time Broichan would believe her when she told him to put no trust in the cunning dwarf. This time he must be banished from Dalriada for ever.

But now was no time for anger. She must concentrate on following the Old Way, which, like the river nearby, writhed and curved and doubled back on itself. Drust claimed that it was his ancestors who had built this track, marking out first each place where there was a firm base of stones or boulders or thick turf, and joining these places with strong carpets of plaited rushes, or tight bundles of peeled willows. He insisted that her people were only carrying on the custom of the race they had conquered by appointing men whose sole work it was to check the Way constantly, and renew such stretches as showed the slightest sign of weakness. Drust . . . Drust . . . time enough to think of him when they came face to face on Dunadd.

She could see it now, the great fortress crowning the hill which reared itself up from the surrounding Moss, but even so she made no attempt to hurry. The reek of the bog gave way imperceptibly to the smell of wood smoke rising from the thatched hall and the huts where Aidan and his men lived. Presently she could make out the guards patrolling the ramparts, but still she watched carefully where she placed each foot. One false step could be fatal, even to the daughter of a goddess.

As she crossed the river at the shallow ford where the bed was paved with flat stones, one of the sentries on the walk above the massive timber gates disappeared, and Bridie knew that he had gone to announce her arrival.

The daughter of a goddess arriving on foot! Her anger mounted.

Brushing past a slave who was struggling to pull his over-laden donkey out of her way, she had only just begun to climb the steep road to the fort when a girl thrust her way through the crowds at the gates and ran towards her. Wide-eyed and sobbing, she threw herself to the ground, clasping Bridie's ankles, while her long dark hair trailed in the mud.

All Bridie's pent-up fear, anger and exasperation spilled over.

"So Danu decided to leave her mistress alone, at the mercy of any wandering robber or murderer, while she enjoyed herself here at Dunadd?" she stormed. Snapping her fingers at a farmer who had herded his sheep and himself against the wall, she pointed to his whip.

Faces peered excitedly over the wooden revetments built on top of the walls leading to the gates; others appeared at various vantage points along the walls of the fortress.

"And Danu left her mistress to journey to Dunadd alone and unaccompanied?"

Bridie seized the proffered whip, but as she raised it in the air a hairy, brown hand grasped her wrist.

"Since when did the daughter of the High One inflict punishment without first finding out if it was deserved?" a curt voice demanded.

Furiously Bridie stared over her shoulder at Drust, not daring to humiliate herself further by struggling against a grip she knew she could not break.

"Tell your gracious mistress why you are here, Danu," Drust said, but Danu only sobbed louder. "Are you afraid that she will beat you for your devotion? Beat you because you nursed her for four days and nights and helped her fight the swamp fever, when it seemed that all Broichan's charms and spells and potions served only to make the malady worse?"

Removing the whip from Bridie's numbed fingers, he tossed it back to the farmer who, frightened, let it fall to the ground.

"Even if what you say is true, it is no excuse for her coming here, and leaving me alone and unattended," Bridie retorted.

"I would never have left you alone, mistress," Danu pleaded, summoning up courage to speak. "Never. Broichan himself assured me that Macha, daughter of Bred, would watch over you until my return."

"But Broichan had much on his mind with the wounds on the prince's left hand, and the calling together of the people from all over Dalriada, to say nothing of the arrangements for the feasting afterwards," Drust added. "It would appear that he forgot to mention the matter to Macha, daughter of Bred. Possibly he did not expect the daughter of the High One to recover so quickly or otherwise he would surely have arranged for her to assist at the crowning of the prince."

Uneasily Bridie glanced from the dwarf's malicious face to the kneeling Danu. There were undercurrents here which she could not fathom.

"Do stop weeping, Danu," she cried, exasperated. "As for you, Drust, guard your tongue. I am sure Broichan can explain everything."

"I am sure he can," Drust agreed, but Bridie felt there was more to his words than their surface meaning.

"Until he has leisure to do so," the dwarf continued, "the goddess will permit me to arrange for her to rest and refresh herself. Naturally she would not dream of exposing herself to the curiosity—even perhaps derision—of her people, by appearing at a ceremony where no provision had been made for her."

"Curiosity? Derision?" Bridie's eyes flashed. "How dare you suggest

that my people . . . that I am not wanted. . . ?" She floundered, unable
to find words to express her wrath. "I shall attend the ceremony as is my
right, and I know that my people will welcome me, whether or not provision has been made for me."

"Daughter of the High One," Drust protested in alarm, "consider
your position . . . your dignity . . . your—"

"I have considered everything, and I am going to the ceremony."

"Your recent illness—"

"Come, Danu."

"At least then, be content to play the role of an onlooker, O daughter
of the High One. If you attempt to interfere a second time, Broichan
will never forgive you."

"Broichan—forgive me?" Bridie could scarcely believe her ears. "It is
I who may never forgive him for holding this feast without my
knowledge and consent."

Drust was frightened now. She could see that. Of course it was
jealousy which had made him speak so foolishly.

"Has the ceremony begun yet?"

A burst of loud cheering and shouting gave her the answer.

"Come, Danu. We must hurry." She paused and looked coldly at the
dwarf. "You too, Drust. There are certain matters we must discuss
—afterwards." And *I prefer you where I can see you*, she thought,
*rather than working more mischief behind my back.*

"The daughter of the goddess is gracious," Drust replied, with a
slight gesture of one hand that might almost have indicated resignation.
"Had I known I was to be so honoured I would have washed my face in
the river, and changed my tunic—except, of course, that this is the only
one I possess."

Disappointed that there was to be no public whipping, the onlookers
had disappeared from the sentry walk and the walls to join the crowds
waiting for the ceremony to begin. Those still making for the gates
—chiefly peasant women and children—pressed against either side of
the approach walls to allow Bridie a clear passage, the more humble and
superstitious closing their eyes tightly lest her glance should annihilate
them.

Followed by Danu and the dwarf, she climbed several flights of stone
steps and arrived at the back of the crowd which thronged the arena in
front of the great carved Rock of the Kings. They were all there, warriors, priests, poets and bards, all resplendent in their ceremonial
armour or robes, all bedecked with glittering jewelry of gold, silver and
bronze, intricately worked and set with precious stones—finger rings,
bracelets, ear-rings, brooches, and round their necks magnificent

torques of twisted gold wire.

Suddenly the shouting and laughter gave way to whispering as the crowd became aware of her presence, and once again everyone made way for her, the bolder and more ambitious praising her beauty, her wisdom and her graciousness, in low but quite audible tones.

If only things had been different, how proud and flattered she would have been. But Drust knew what he had been doing when he sowed those seeds of doubt. Was there curiosity and derision in the sidelong glances of the crowd? He was right. She should never have come. She should have spared herself this humiliation of wondering what everyone was thinking. No! Why should she allow herself to be upset by the dwarf's malice?

Proudly she lifted up her head. She was Brigid, the daughter of the High One. Broichan was her high priest and loved her above all others. This was not the first time Drust had tried to come between them, but it would certainly be the last. Although it was too late now to take part in the ceremony, she could give it her approval by watching it.

A great shout of excitement rang out as Broichan stepped out from the Great Hall, leading the prince forward with solemn dignity. How pale Aidan's face was, Bridie thought, how glazed his eyes, as he stared over the heads of his people to the distant mountains, but how magnificent he looked, the sunlight glinting on the golden helmet and breastplate fashioned long ago by the dark gods of the underworld. Finer than those of any of the warriors were the snake bracelets on his arms, the engraved and jewelled rings on his right hand, and the torque with its pattern of entwined birds and beasts—the same fantastic creatures as were embroidered on the robe she herself was now wearing. Only his left hand was unadorned, bound as it was with a linen bandage and supported in a sling.

Splendid in his yellow woollen robe besprinkled with gold and silver, his bull's hide cloak and his magnificent head-dress of birds' feathers, Broichan paused, and then slowly knelt on the flat rock and with his forefinger traced the engraved outline of the boar—the symbol for the Celts of all that was valiant and virile.

Chanting the invocation to the Great White One, Broichan rose to his feet, waited until Kenneth (almost as pale as his prince) had filled the rock hollow with water and unfastened Aidan's sandal, and then, kneeling again, he bathed the prince's foot before leading him to the footprint which marked the exact place where the first of the kings of Dalriada had stood when he was crowned, and although Bridie willed Broichan to look across at her and acknowledge her presence, never once did he look in her direction.

Something was wrong.

The prince moved as though he had no idea where he was or what he was doing. Kenneth was so frightened that he could hardly control the trembling of his hands. Even Broichan was different in some way. His voice did not ring out as magnificently as usual, so that for once, what he said was more important than the manner in which he said it. Those splendid gestures which hypnotized the crowd were but token movements. And why did he keep glancing at the left hand of the prince, enclosed in its linen sling?

Of course.

The great amber betrothal ring, given so long ago by her mother, the High One, and worn by her kings since the beginnings of time. How was he to place it on Aidan's finger as law and custom demanded?

He will unwrap the bandage and make a token gesture of placing the ring on the injured hand, she told herself as Broichan began the invocation to her mother. But when the long chant came to an end, Aidan's hand was still in its sling and Broichan was passing without a break to invoke the help of the Nameless Ones of Dunadd.

Broichan had forgotten, genuinely forgotten, Bridie pleaded with her doubting self. But the whole ceremony will be invalid unless someone reminds him.

"The ring!" she whispered, as loudly as she dared, and then, as Broichan evidently had not heard, she stepped forward. "Can you not keep your mouth closed for once?" Drust whispered, pulling her back. "Wait until the ceremony is over and then quarrel with Broichan about your ring." Wrenching her arm free, Bridie slapped Drust across the face and then ran across to the high priest. "The ring!" she cried in a voice that all could hear.

Turning, Broichan threw her one single, furious glance.

"Be quiet!" he ordered, and with his back to her once more, he continued smoothly with his intoning.

For a moment Bridie stood there, unable to believe her ears, and then she felt herself in the grip of a greater anger than she had ever experienced. No one, not even her high priest, could speak to her like that.

"Stop the ceremony at once!" she shouted, and hurrying forward, she placed herself between the priest and the prince, just as Kenneth was guiding Aidan's foot to the carved print and Broichan was lifting the gold circlet to place on his corn-yellow hair.

"No man can be crowned King of Dalriada unless the high priest has first placed on the third finger of his left hand the great amber betrothal ring which was given to our people long ago by my mother, the High One, and which has been worn by our kings since the beginning of time.

That is the law of my people and no high priest can alter it."

Stiff and erect, Aidan stared at the rolling clouds which hid the mountains, and said nothing. He can neither see nor hear, Bridie thought, and then she saw the terrible fury in Broichan's dark eyes—a naked, murderous hate such as she had never known existed in any man —and she would have turned and fled, had she not been hemmed in by the whispering, jostling crowd.

Terrified, she wanted to cry out that it was Drust who had put the ideas in her head: that of course she loved and trusted him, but before she could find the words Broichan's face cleared and he was looking down at her with his old familiar, easy smile. Placing one arm round her shoulders, he drew her to him, so that now they both faced the excited crowd.

"Listen to what I have to say, you mighty men of Dalriada," he cried. "You warriors were witness to the fearless manner in which your prince fought. So gravely was he wounded that it seemed the gods had called him, along with our king and other warriors, to Tir-nan-Og." As he paused there was the rattle of armour as the men moved to exchange whispered comments. "But I invoked the Great White One himself, and when he declared the auguries favourable, then with my magic and skill and knowledge, I healed the prince—every wound except one spear thrust in the left hand.

"Would you see your prince standing before you, blood dripping from an unhealed wound, because of a ceremony which has long lost its meaning?

"Right hand, or left, what does it matter?

"We are not ignorant, fearful creatures like our ancestors. We are a great and growing people, ready to change our customs to make ourselves even greater.

"The High One helped us in the old days when men knew little of the land in which they lived, or the enemies who surrounded them. But for a powerful people such as we are, we need a god like the Great White One who can inspire us to make Dalriada the greatest—the only —kingdom in this country."

Frenzedly the younger men cheered and shouted, but they were careful not to look at Bridie, for as yet they had no reason not to fear her. Although many of them resented power being in the hands of women (whether the women were queens, goddesses, soothsayers or seers) they could not forget that it was Brigid who had warned them against defeat, and they had paid dearly for ignoring her warning.

"Why do you say that you healed the prince," Bridie demanded, "when it was the Healer from the Unborn Years who gave him his blood?"

The fingers on her shoulder closed like pincers and, just as suddenly, relaxed.

"We all grieved when the Marsh People cast a spell on the daughter of the High One," Broichan said in solicitous tones. "No one—not even I, with all my experience—expected her to make such a quick recovery, and while we admire the devotion to her people which brought her, tired and sick, to this ceremony, yet she would have been better advised to rest until she learned to distinguish between nightmares and reality. It was I, and I alone, who healed your prince."

She recalled how strangely young Congus had looked at her when she asked about the Healer. Was the Healer really only a ghost from the long hours when the Marsh People had stolen her memory? Was it true she could not distinguish between nightmares and reality? And yet it seemed to her that she could see him now; the Healer in his strange clothes, kneeling by Aidan as he unwrapped the bandage, and Broichan drawing her aside and asking her to go to the House of Secrets for the blue phial with the silver stopper.

She stiffened. Had she for one moment seen the hand and at the same time not seen it, because she was concentrating on Broichan's instructions, because the priest had turned her away before she could be sure?

"Aidan," she cried in anguish, "if you love your people and your honour, unwrap the bandage from your left hand so that Broichan can place the betrothal ring on your finger." But the prince stared ahead, unheeding, and Bridie knew that Broichan had shown him the swinging golden charm of the Great White One, and had taken from him both his will and his memory; but whether it was to help him bear the pain of his wounds or to endure the long ceremony in his present weakness, she did not know.

"Kenneth," she urged, "if you love your foster-brother and value his honour and your own, draw your dagger and cut the bandage from his left hand."

Fingering the ivory hilt of his dagger, Kenneth looked fearfully at Broichan, but before he could make any move Bridie knocked his hand aside, seized the weapon herself and cut first the sling and then the bandaging and finally eased off the dressing of sphagnum moss.

In the front rank the warriors and chief men caught their breath, incredulous, horrified; behind them others shoved and pushed, their weapons and armour clashing, their ceremonial jewelry ringing and jingling as they pressed forward, the better to see.

And then the muttering and whispering began, growing louder and angrier and more and more threatening, until the shouts and cries were taken up on all sides:

"The prince has lost two fingers!"

"No man who is physically blemished can be our king."

"It does not matter how valiant he is in single combat or in battle, Aidan is no longer perfect, and only the perfect man can rule us."

"Only the perfect man can rule us. This has always been our law and it is a law that can never be changed."

"Silence!" Broichan shouted furiously. "Silence!"

The cries faded to mutterings and finally died away, but there was no doubt about the suspicion and unease amongst the crowd.

"Do you think that I, Broichan, your high priest, do not know that my work of healing your prince is not yet finished? To create two new fingers is not beyond my power, but time is needed.

"When I sought advice from the Great White One concerning the crowning of your prince, all the propitious omens and auguries were for this day and this hour and this place. I tell you that it will be many moons before such a favourable time again occurs, and a people as great as you are must have a king to make decisions and protect you from your enemies.

"Because of this, I say the ceremony must continue. Afterwards you will feast and drink and listen to the music of the harp, and hear the heroic exploits of our brave ancestors. During this time I shall intercede with the Great White One, who may perhaps advise that not all old laws must remain unchanged in a young and powerful kingdom such as Dalriada."

Another few minutes, Bridie thought, and Broichan would have won them over with his eloquence and authority. Beside her Drust, one cheek still scarlet from the slap she had administered, was trying to persuade her to say nothing more, to leave matters as they were, to trust Broichan, who would explain everything later. But that would be too late. Broichan was wrong, just as he had been over the last battle: she was right, and pride insisted that she must force him to admit it.

"It is my turn to speak to my people, Broichan," she said, freeing herself of his restraining arm. "I Brigid, daughter of the High One, know that the Celtic peoples have had many gods and goddesses to whom they have turned for their different needs.

"The Great White One, through Broichan, has always cared for my warriors in battle, because they have worshipped him, sacrificed to him. And the Great White One decrees that the ceremony of crowning must be held today.

"But my mother, the High One, has also looked after you. The mother of each man here called out to her for her help at the moment of his birth: the wife of each man here received her help when his children were born. It is my mother who will guide each one of you when the moment comes for you to leave this world for the long journey to Tir-nan-Og."

She paused, and when she began again, she spoke very slowly, emphasizing every word.

"And so I warn each one of you that I, the daughter of the High One, accept as king of my people no man, however brave, who does not wear my betrothal ring on the third finger of his left hand: and if any man, be he warrior or priest, disregards my words, I prophesy that sickness and disaster will overtake all my people, and the great, black, screaming night-bird of death will pursue them until their leaders cry to me for mercy and acknowledge their most grievous error."

And lifting her peat-stained sandalled foot, Bridie placed it in the engraved footprint and stared defiantly at Broichan.

No one moved. No one spoke. Every man knew that if their king, or any of their leaders, broke any of the tribal laws, the whole tribe would suffer. It had happened in the past to their forefathers: it could happen again—to them.

Broichan knew when he was beaten. He also knew that somehow defeat must be turned into victory. Boasts and wild prophecies were what his people needed and expected: boasts and prophecies they should have.

"The daughter of the High One, young and inexperienced as she is, must be right," he said, with only the faintest suspicion of doubt in his tone. "But the preparations for the feast are made, and the women are waiting in the Great Hall to pour mead. Go now and celebrate, and while you rejoice, I shall make the greatest magic of all.

"I promise you this, O mighty warriors of Dalriada, that on the seventh day after this, when the feast comes to an end, I shall return to you with your prince, and the daughter of the High One shall, herself, place the amber engagement ring on the new finger which I shall have fashioned, and then I, Broichan, your high priest, whose knowledge and skill and learning was born of the magic and supernatural forces of the Other-world, I, Broichan, will crown Aidan, king of Dalriada."

# 7   The Especially Sacred Forest

WHEN THEY reached the mangled, uprooted ash tree, the pony shied, whinnying in terror, and not all Bridie's commands or coaxing could persuade it to take another step. By the time she had decided she'd have to walk across the causeway to her dwelling and had dismounted, Danu had caught up with her.

"Well," she said aggressively, after a fleeting glance at her slave's troubled face, "what is the matter now? I know you never believed the mountain ash would protect my home, so why should you be so upset because the wild swine have savaged it?"

Danu swallowed, but made no attempt to answer.

"Perhaps you have lost your faith in your priest Columba and his new God, as neither of them appears to have shown any interest in you. Perhaps you have come to fear the Great White One because his creatures did this?" She gestured towards the tree that had so delighted her eye with its dark green leaves and red, bead-like berries.

"No, mistress, I have not lost my faith in the new God of the Prince Columba. And it is not I who believe in, or fear, the Great White One."

"I do not understand you, Danu. I certainly do not fear him either. My mother is far more powerful than he."

"Yes, mistress."

Bridie was silent. In spite of what she had said, she knew, just as her pony had done, that now there was neither safety nor protection for her in her island home.

"It is not what has happened to the ash tree that troubles me, mistress," Danu burst out. "Why did you act as you did in the fortress of Dunadd, O daughter of the High One? To expose the—the deceit of your prince and your high priest in front of the chief men among your people! Broichan will never forgive you."

Bridie shrugged her shoulders.

"Of course he will forgive me. He knows what I did was right. Just as I was right when I warned him not to fight. All will be well between us in a week's time, when he has made the new fingers." She hesitated.

"But why did Broichan pretend that nothing was wrong? And Aidan too?

"There are many things that I do not understand, but I mean to find out the answers for myself, Danu, and first of all, I am going to talk to the prince."

"You know that is impossible, mistress. Broichan has taken him to the Place of Healing and given orders that nobody is to be admitted while he works his healing magic."

"Drust and Kenneth are with him, and I have always gone and come as I wanted. Broichan will not stop me now. We shall go there at once."

Nothing would make her admit how glad she was to have a reason for not trying to cross the loch to her dwelling: what was to happen to her later she had no idea, but she knew with a sad certainty that she would never live in her island home again.

As they remounted their ponies, she glanced anxiously at the sky. As so often happened at this season, the wind was increasing in strength with the approach of sunset and bringing with it the threat of more rain. Before very long she would have to decide where they were to spend the night if Broichan would not admit her to the Place of Healing. But that was ridiculous and she refused even to think about it. More to the point would be to decide how she should treat the high priest when they met again.

Should she perhaps weep and say she was sorry? But she was not sorry. What she had done had been right. That brief taste of power when she had harangued her people was still sweet in her memory. Never again must Broichan forget she was the daughter of a goddess.

She was still undecided about her approach as they reined their horses in front of the closed gates, and saw the figure huddled against one of the posts.

"Kenneth! What are you doing here? What has happened?"

The boy lifted a tear-stained face.

"Broichan has taken my foster-brother inside to make him perfect once more. He is working his most terrible magic, that would kill me if I saw or heard it. And so I am waiting."

"Out here? For how long?"

"Until the seventh day, when my foster-brother comes out with his new fingers."

"And where is Drust? Inside, I suppose."

"No. Broichan quarrelled with him, or he quarrelled with Broichan, I do not know which. He has gone away, cursing and swearing. But he will come back. They often quarrel, Broichan and Drust, and Drust goes off, but he always comes back in the end."

"Poor Kenneth!" Bridie sat on the ground beside the boy and put her arm round him. "You cannot stay here for seven days and nights without food or shelter. I shall tell Broichan he must let you in. You will be quite safe with us in one of the dormitories."

"You do not understand, goddess. Broichan will not open the gates to anyone, not even to you. And if he did say that I might enter, I dare not set foot in the Place of Healing again."

His terror was beginning to communicate itself to her, but she knew she had to remain confident if ever she was to resolve her growing doubts.

"Kenneth," she said, lowering her voice, "do you believe that Broichan really can make new fingers?" When the boy kept his head averted and made no attempt to reply, she tried again. "Did your foster-brother know that he had lost two fingers in battle?"

Kenneth sighed, as though it were a question he both dreaded and welcomed.

"That is what I have asked myself over and over again, goddess. When he was carried here from the battlefield he was unconscious and did not know about it. Perhaps he saw his hand when the Healer looked at it. I do not know. But if so, he forgot. I will swear he forgot. Never once did he refer to it or ask to have the dressing removed."

"But Broichan knew as soon as the prince was brought here?"

"Yes."

"Who else?"

"I did."

"But you told no one?"

"No. Broichan forbade me to speak of it. He said he would send for a Healer from the Unborn Years, who would make new fingers so that no one should know they had been lost."

Bridie was silent. Broichan had lied when he said, in front of all her people, that she confused nightmares with reality. There had been a Healer. Why had Broichan denied his existence?

"Did anyone else know about the prince's hand, Kenneth?"

"Drust. He knows everything."

"Any of the warriors?"

"Taran and Dungal, who were fighting beside the chariot and saw the sword blow. They died later of their wounds."

"Here, in the Place of Healing?"

"Yes."

"I do not know what to say or what to think," Bridie said slowly. One by one the terrible doubts at the back of her mind were coming forward and identifying themselves. "The prince himself, who must have seen he had lost two fingers—and then forgot. Two warriors who saw, and died. Drust, who saw and said nothing, because he is Broichan's slave and bodyguard and counsellor. You, Kenneth, who saw and said nothing, because you were afraid. Was there anyone else?"

"The Healer from the Unborn Years."

"Of course. And what happened to him?"

"He returned to his own time."

"How do you know?"

"Broichan told me." He began to cry again. "I am so frightened—for the prince as well as for myself. If I were not Aidan's foster-brother, and my father a king, I know that I should now be dead like Taran and Dungal. I think that you can aid me, Brigid, even though I do not worship you or your mother. Please help me to return to my home in Ireland and to take my foster-brother with me. The God I worship asks for love, not blood sacrifices, and Columba, our priest, does not expect our king to be perfect."

Impulsively Bridie kissed the boy, glad to feel herself important again.

"You shall return to your people and worship in your own way, Kenneth. I promise you that. There is just one more question." And this, she knew, was the most crucial of all. "Was there any way you could tell the prince and the Healer apart?"

"Not after they became blood-brothers, and the Healer began to understand and speak our language."

"Strange questions for the daughter of a goddess to ask!" A shadow, grotesque and misshapen, detached itself from the darkness of the forest and Kenneth, with a cry of fright, pulled himself away from Bridie and ran to Danu, who held out her arms to him and murmured softly, reassuringly. "But why stop there?" Drust continued, sidling up to Bridie. "Surely there are other, even more interesting questions to occupy the mind—hitherto concerned only with herself—of the Gracious One?

"Perhaps she wonders whether the Healer has indeed returned to his own time? And why Broichan publicly disclaimed all knowledge of him?

"Perhaps she wonders if Broichan plumbed some secret ambition, unknown to the Healer, to be a leader of men, and is preparing him, either with or without his knowledge and consent, to take the place of the now maimed prince?

"Alas! What would Broichan say if he knew the thoughts of the goddess he once worshipped—or was it perhaps the goddess, in her youth and ignorance, who worshipped him?"

"How long have you been hiding there, listening?" Bridie asked fearfully.

"Long enough, goddess. Long enough."

"And now, I suppose, you will go back to your master and tell him not just what I have said but what I have thought," she said bitterly. "This is the chance you have waited for. You have always hated me and sneered at me. You have always tried to turn Broichan against me. Why? What harm have I ever done you?"

"Mistress," Danu cried, looking over Kenneth's head, "you are wrong, and even though you have me beaten, I must have my say.

"Drust has never hated you. The fault was yours. Because his outside did not please you, you never paused to discover the man inside. You provoked his sharp tongue with your dislike. You were jealous when Broichan listened to his wisdom instead of taking your inexperienced advice.

"When your warriors took me prisoner and brought me here to Dalriada—I, who was the daughter of a king—it was Drust who comforted me and helped me to bear the lot of a slave. When I wept for my parents and brothers who were slain by your army, it was Drust who dried my tears and taught me to find consolation where I thought to find none again.

"You do not know Drust, mistress, and the loss is yours, if only you realized it."

"You, the daughter of a king?" Bridie was taken aback. "I . . . I did not know. You should have told me. Drust should have told me." Because Broichan had rescued her from a poor herdsman's dwelling, she was now the daughter of a goddess, and Danu, once a princess, was her slave. She was bitterly ashamed of herself and the way she had treated the patient girl. "I am sorry, Danu. Somehow I will make amends. I promise you that. But whatever you say of Drust, I tell you this: he serves only one master, and that master is Broichan."

"No, mistress. He serves Aidan, the prince, and has done so always. Only as long as Broichan is loyal to the prince will Drust serve him."

Uncertainly, Bridie looked at the dwarf.

"Is this true, Drust?"

"It is true."

"Danu trusts you because you have been kind to her. She always sees the best in people. But how do I know if I can believe you?"

"How can you afford not to believe me?"

In the ugly face, the green eyes beneath the straggling red hair, Bridie could find no reassurance.

"I do not know what to think . . . " she began, but Drust interrupted her curtly.

"You mean you know only too well what you think, but you are afraid to put it into words. So I shall do it for you, and you will listen, because you are listening to your own thoughts.

"Broichan is young for a high priest. He is good-looking, clever and ambitious. He is supported by those among the warriors who are also young and ambitious.

"These warriors want to fight many battles. They want personal glory and the spoils of war: land, possessions, and slaves to work for them. Aidan has always been their hero, because he too is young, brave and ambitious. And he has always accepted Broichan's counsel.

"But when Aidan lost two fingers in battle, and the Healer from the Unborn Years said he could not replace them, Aidan refused to be crowned king. He said he would be breaking the ancient law of the Celts and would bring ill-luck and misfortune on all his people. Aidan, you see, is a man of honour as well of ambition.

"Broichan puts ambition first. For him, it was essential that Aidan should be king. I agreed. Of all the warriors, he is the best fitted for leadership. Broichan therefore showed him the swinging golden charm of the Great White One, and looked deeply into Aidan's eyes until he had taken away the prince's will and imposed his own, so that Aidan now obeys only Broichan.

"Our plan was simple. Aidan should be made king, and while the older warriors and chief men feasted, Aidan would lead a picked band of his followers in a surprise raid on the Britons whose land adjoins ours. This time we would win as the tribe is split by the struggle for power of two of the warriors, and Broichan has arrranged to fight with the more powerful section as allies. In the general rejoicing afterwards and the sharing of the loot and plunder, the young men would press for the law of physical perfection to be changed, and Broichan would see that it was.

"It was a good plan. Good for Aidan and his people. A king is none the less a king because he lacks two fingers, just as a man is none the less a man because his body is crooked."

Bridie dropped her eyes because she could not bear to look at Drust now, so frightened and ashamed was she.

"It was a good plan, and all would have gone well, except that you, goddess, recovered too quickly from your marsh fever and attended the ceremony when we hoped you were safely out of the way.

"Out of injured pride and childish pique, you challenged Broichan's authority. With your own hands you revealed the extent of Aidan's injury; and the people, unprepared and shocked, rejected him.

"In desperation, Broichan promised them the impossible. But, Brigid, within seven days they will have the impossible. They will have a prince with new fingers." Drust brought his face, distorted with fury, close to Bridie's. "A prince similar in face and figure and ambition to Aidan, but who is not Aidan.''

"The Healer?" She swallowed. "And . . . Aidan?"

"There is no longer any place for Aidan in Broichan's plans. Tonight Broichan will offer the prince as a sacrifice to the Great White One, in return for the help of the god. One man must die for the good of the people, so Broichan says, but what he means is that Aidan must die so that he can retain his power as high priest.

"But I, Drust, say that Aidan must die only because of the foolish pride of a foolish child!''

"Oh, no, no, no," Bridie whispered. "I did not know. How could I know?" She turned to Danu and Kenneth to ask them to believe her and then turned back, unable to face their grief and fear. "Tonight?" she asked.

"Tonight. Before the sun sets Broichan will send Aidan alone into the Especially Sacred Forest. And what chance do you think he will have, unarmed and drugged, to escape from the Great White One?"

"I would go with him, and defend him with my dagger," Kenneth burst out, still holding Danu's hand for comfort, "but I am afraid of the Great White One, and ashamed of being afraid.''

"We will go together, Kenneth," Bridie cried, searching desperately for the courage which she had once thought she possessed. "You will be safe with me, the daughter of the High One." Slowly confidence was seeping back. If she had made mistakes, then somehow she must put matters right. Nothing was impossible for the daughter of a goddess.

Beckoning to Danu, she took from her forefinger her coiled-bronze snake ring, the head set with eyes of green glass, and held it out.

"Danu, the past is past, and cannot be undone. I know now that I have been unkind and thoughtless, and I am truly sorry. Dalriada is no place for you. Take this ring and ride as fast as you can to your own people in the far north, where you can live once more as a princess should. If any guards challenge you, or any scouts intercept you, show them this ring, and say you are on a mission for me, and you will be safe. Now go."

Danu stared at her beseechingly.

"Do not send me away by myself, Brigid. Like Kenneth, I am afraid although I have never worshipped your gods, I am afraid of the Marsh People, of the grey men who rise by night from the stone houses in lonely places, of the cruel horses who live at the bottom of the lochs, and the terrible hags who bestride the mountain tops. Let me stay here with you, Brigid."

"It is your freedom I am offering you," Bridie cried impatiently, forcing the ring into the unwilling hand. "Go at once." And she turned away lest she be haunted by the fear and unhappiness in Danu's eyes.

"Do not stare at me like that!" she stormed at Kenneth. "Congus will give her provisions at the Fort of the Strangers. She will come to no harm."

Not until the clatter of the pony's hoofs had been lost in the buffeting of the wind and the creaking of branches did anyone speak.

"Danu will come to no harm," Bridie repeated. "Now we must rescue the prince."

"How?" Drust asked curtly. "We do not know where or when Aidan will enter the Especially Sacred Forest. We do know he will go straight to the sanctuary. Doubtless the goddess is familiar with the path there?"

"You know I am not. No one has ever set foot in the Forest except those whom the god calls for sacrifice. Only the high-priest comes and goes in safety."

"And I," Drust said softly. "I, who am the last of my race, the last of those who lived here before the Celtic tribes began their long journey from the East." He waited. Despise me and distrust me, his mocking smile said, but if you want my help, humble yourself to ask for it.

"Will you lead me to the sanctuary, Drust?"

"For what reason, Brigid?"

"I have endangered the prince's life. Now I must save it."

"Brave words. You have seen the god?"

Bridie shook her head. Only Broichan had seen the god and lived, but everyone knew how terrible he was.

"And when you do come face to face with him, what will you do?"

"Ask him to spare the prince's life."

Drust stared at her incredulously, and then burst out into mocking laughter.

"My mother will help me when the time comes," Bridie cried, stung by this open derision.

"It would be advisable to have more than a mother to rely on when facing the Great White One, Brigid. If you want my help, you must decide whether or not you can trust me. You do not need to like me."

"How can I trust you when I still do not know if you have told me the truth? I cannot see why Aidan must die just because he has lost two fingers. You yourself said he refuses now to be king. He would be well content to fight under his cousin, Maelcon, who would be our next king."

"But Broichan will not allow Maelcon to be king," Kenneth interrupted. "Maelcon was taught by Columba and worships my God, mine and Danu's. If Maelcon is king, there will be no place for the old gods, or for their high-priest, Broichan. That is why he plans to kill Aidan and put the Healer in his place."

The wind moaned in the tree tops and a large bat swooped down within a few inches of their heads and disappeared behind the palisade of the Place of Healing.

"I think I understand now," Bridie said at length. "Drust, tell me what I can do to save Aidan, and I will do it."

"At last!" the dwarf said. He opened the leather pouch hanging from his belt to check that its contents were safe, and then drew his iron dagger from its sheath, testing first one edge and then the other with a calloused thumb before replacing it. "I shall lead the way. Follow the goddess, Kenneth, and do not let your hand stray far from the handle of your dagger."

The pale stars died away as heavy black clouds raced across the sky, and the trees in the wood tossed and creaked in the wind as the three figures made their way through the darkness of the forest.

Was she right to trust the dwarf, Bridie asked herself. She knew how smoothly he could lie when it suited him. Once they were far enough from the Place of Healing, would he turn on her and slay her and Kenneth with that wicked dagger he had caressed so lovingly? It was Broichan she should trust. He would be able to explain everything. She would not go another step. She would tell Drust. But before she had got any further in her thoughts, the dwarf twisted round and thrust her violently sideways into the dank undergrowth.

"Save me!" she wanted to cry as Kenneth fell beside her. "Save us both!"

It was only in the very moment of falling, when the foetid breath fanned her cheek, and the slobbering, fanged mouth grazed her ear that she realized the enemy was not Drust, but one of Broichan's great hunting dogs, trained to attack and kill without warning.

Crouching among thorns and nettles, one leg bent awkwardly under her, she listened to the laboured breathing, the crash of snapping branches, the scuffling amongst dead leaves. Suddenly a high-pitched scream filled the darkness and was cut off abruptly, to be followed by a soft, bubbling, choking cough. Then there was only the terrible sound of laboured breathing, the voice of the wind and the muted cries of the forest.

"Drust?"

"Wait."

They waited as the harsh breathing was forced under control.

"All is well. We can go on now. Come."

"Are you hurt, Drust?" Kenneth asked anxiously.

"A scratch here and there. Nothing that matters."

"What was Broichan's hound doing here, alone?" Bridie asked, trying to ignore the pain of her numbed leg, the virulent nettle poison spreading through her arm.

Drust laughed bitterly.

"Broichan leaves nothing to chance. He sent the hound with Aidan to make sure he entered the Especially Sacred Forest. When a young man comes to the end of his span in this world, even though his reason is taken from him, something within him can warn him so that he twists and fights to escape his fate."

Branches brushed against their faces and arms, briars tried to entangle their legs as, breathless, they climbed the steeply sloping ground after the dwarf.

If she had been a child, Bridie thought, she could have screamed, or run away, or pretended nothing had happened. But she was no longer a child: screaming would achieve nothing; she had done with pretence, and there was no one to run to.

There were two terrible facts she had to face. The first was that the man who had meant most to her all her life was prepared to kill his king to serve his own ends; the second that she was about to set foot on forbidden ground, to enter a forest sacred to a god far more cruel and ruthless than her mother. Not even the bravest of her warriors would come anywhere near the Especially Sacred Forest, and it was whispered that Broichan himself entered it only when the god was somnolent after over-eating.

She was going to plead with this god to spare Aidan's life. But supposing he said no? Supposing he refused even to listen to her? Even though she were the daughter of a goddess, what could she do?

She stiffened as Drust stretched back a restraining hand, abandoning the future to concentrate on the immediate present. The warning hand withdrew, and a moment later she could hear it moving lightly over stone and then wood, and she knew that they must have come to the palisaded wall which enclosed the Especially Sacred Forest.

A heavy wooden gate creaked open.

"From here to the top of the hill, the Forest belongs to the Great White One," Drust said. "Do you want to run away?" For the first time there was no mockery in his tone.

"Yes," Bridie answered. "but there is some reason why I cannot," and she entered the Forest and, sick with fear, listened as the gate closed behind them.

Higher they climbed and higher.

"We have plenty of time," Drust said. "The Great White One never wakens before midnight. If all goes well we should be clear of the Forest long before that—and the prince with us."

The fresh smell of bark and sap and green leaves had gone now: there was no movement of birds in the topmost branches of the trees, of small animals in the undergrowth. Had the wind not blown so fiercely, the stench would have been unbearable.

"This is an evil place," Kenneth whispered. "I hate it."

"You must not say that about the home of our god," Bridie said, frightened at the sudden realization that it was her own thoughts the boy was voicing.

"The Great White One is not my god. My God does not kill people. He asks us to love Him, not to fear Him."

The ground now was soft and churned up, so that Bridie found it more difficult with each step to pull her feet free of the foul, clinging mud.

"Just ahead of us is a great black rock with hand and foot holds," Drust began, when lightning forked across the sky, and for the first time Bridie saw the shrine and sanctuary of the Great White One, the god of her people. Long after the darkness closed in and the thunder pealed and rolled, she could still see it in all its sickening detail.

On either side of the wooden shrine was a semi-circle of massive tree trunks shorn of their leaves and branches and crudely carved to represent some terrible nightmare aspect of the god. One was headless, its glass eyes and leering mouth set in its chest; the head of another was all gaping mouth set with three rows of pointed teeth; a third had monstrous hands which tore apart the limbs of its human victim. Each wooden statue was adorned with human skulls and stained with the blood of victims sacrificed throughout countless years.

Crouching in supplication before the shrine, and in an area of trampled mud and slime, was the prince.

"Say nothing!" Drust whispered sharply. "Listen to me and do exactly as I say and all will be well.

"Brigid—climb to the top of that rock in front of you and wait there until I need you.

"Kenneth—if you have any faith in that God of yours, then invoke His help now. I stake all on the prince recognizing your voice and on your love for him. Go to him and say, 'Aidan, I am Kenneth, your foster-brother. Broichan has sent me to lead you to the Great White One who waits on the top of the rock.' Take his hand and help him to climb the rock to Brigid and then climb up after him. I shall wait below to make sure you are both safe. Go now."

Her heart hammering painfully, Bridie clawed at the holds in the rock, tearing her dress and bruising her fingers in panic; she had just gained the top when the sanctuary was lit up again.

Drust and Kenneth were making their way with difficulty through the mud: Aidan still crouched in front of the shrine—but he was no longer alone.

Evil-smelling, bad-tempered at being awakened so early by the thunder, the Great White One had emerged from his lair in the Forest. Head lowered, his one remaining eye—the other lost years before in the fight which established his supremacy—reflecting the lightning just as did the glass eyes of the wooden statues, the huge boar squealed and snorted in his wrath, waiting for his victim to shriek and flee, so that he might enjoy the pleasure of the chase as well as of the kill.

Great he certainly was; bigger and heavier than any boar Bridie had ever known. White he might once, have been, but very recently he had wallowed in a bath of mud which had set over his bristles into an iron-hard coat, one that no dagger could penetrate.

"The gods are against us," Drust muttered. "Now I must fight with my hands like a mere warrior when tongue and wits have always been my weapons. When I say 'Now!' carry out your part, Kenneth." From his pouch he drew a sling of bone and leather, fitted into it a sharp-edged flint, and waited.

When once more the lightning was reflected from the only vulnerable point of that armour-encased body, he took aim, and the stone found its mark, deep in the boar's right eye.

At first the beast stood there, unable to comprehend what had happened, and then, squealing in agony it rolled over, trying to bury its head in the mud in an effort to lessen the pain.

"Now!" Drust commanded, and Kenneth plunged forward.

"Aidan," he cried, tugging at the prince's arm, "I am Kenneth, your foster-brother. Broichan has sent me to lead you to the Great White One who waits on the top of the rock."

Not daring to breath, Bridie listened. There was no answer from Aidan, but she could hear him get to his feet, hear two people stumble through the clinging mud and immediately she was on her knees, waiting to help them climb up the rock.

"You are safe!" she cried. "Oh, Kenneth, you are safe."

Stretching out a timid hand, she touched Aidan, but there was no response, and she knew it was only his shell that was with them. Drust would help him to become a whole man again, she thought, desperately trying to allay her own fears; but Drust was below, making no attempt to seek safety for himself.

"Drust, come up at once," she shouted. The boar might now be blind, but sight, she knew, was always the least important of any creature's senses.

"He cannot come here," Kenneth said, angry at her stupidity and ashamed at the little he could do. "I have heard the old men talk of this rock. It is called the Rock of the Victims. The Great White One knows it well. He knows that without food or water a man can stay here only so long. At last, weak and feeble, he must come down—to find the boar waiting for him.

"Drust knows he has to kill the beast while we have strength enough to escape. But it is not a dwarf who should be fighting. That is the work of Aidan, the prince and warrior."

Beside them Aidan stood stiff and silent, and they knew he heard nothing, not even the thunder which rolled and crashed over the hills and the Great Moss of Dalriada.

Now Bridie could smell human blood, and she remembered, with a sinking heart, that Drust had been injured when he killed the hunting dog: wherever he moved the boar would follow him with his nose and ears. He would wait until Drust tired himself out, and then. . . .

Drust's laboured breathing was much farther away now, and the next flash of lightning revealed him on the roof of the shrine, slicing at the roped stones which prevented the gales from tearing off the thatch. Just before the scene was blotted out she saw him lift a heavy stone in both hands and hurl it on to the beast below. Above the maddened creature's squealing she heard Drust's hoarse shout of triumph as he leaped to the ground, and then the cry changed to a groan that was lost in the grunting of the boar.

"Drust!" Kenneth cried, and when there was no answer, "Drust! Are you hurt?" But all they could hear was the fury of the boar as it struggled to its feet.

"He is injured—unconscious." Angry and frightened, he turned to Bridie. "You are supposed to be the daughter of a goddess: why do you not do something to help him? Do something! You see, there is nothing you can do, is there?

"What fools your people are, to believe a girl is the daughter of a goddess and a pig is a god! As for your prince—a fine hero he is." His voice broke. He could not bear to think of the foster-brother he had idolized doing nothing when they were in such danger. "Drust is worth a hundred of you, and if I cannot save him, I shall die beside him." And he was gone into the darkness below.

In an agony of despair Bridie began to weep, knowing that injured and sightless as the boar was, it would easily outwit and kill the inexperienced boy.

Was Kenneth right in what he had said? The prince was no hero. The

Great White One was a boar. But she?

If she were only a girl, Drust would never have brought her here to rescue the prince. He could have worked better alone. No—he knew that the time would come when he would need those special powers possessed only by the daughter of a goddess. And now, surely, that time had come. The fact that the High One had no time to help her own daughter did not mean that Brigid should neglect her responsibilities.

As far back as folk memory stretched, the Celtic people had worshipped the High One, the great Earth Mother: the goddess had chosen her, Brigid, to care for the people of Dalriada. Whether Kenneth believed in her or not, it was her duty to save them all from the evil creature below.

Standing erect and throwing back her long hair, she called out imperiously:

"I, Brigid, daughter of the High One, command the starheart of the storm and the wind, the rain and the thunder and lightning to help me now. Save the lives of Drust the Dwarf and of Kenneth who has gone to help him. Bring back reason to the empty shell of our prince. I command you to help us now!"

High overhead the thunder reverberated and tongues of white fire licked the trees on the summit of the hill. For a moment all was dark, and then the fire sprang to life again, now blood red and gold.

I am indeed the daughter of a goddess, Bridie exulted, as the gale fanned the leaping flames and they began to spread downhill, while below, the defiant Kenneth taunted the boar with mirthless laughter, in an effort to divert it from the crumpled figure of the dwarf.

Head lowered and twisted sideways, the boar waited . . . and then charged. As he tried to leap out of its path, Kenneth slipped in the mud and the cruel tusk ripped open the sleeve of his jerkin, and the arm underneath.

"Oh, no!" Bridie whispered. "Save him, High One. Please save him."

For a moment she thought someone answered in a strange language, but when the cry was repeated, she realized it came from the shrine and was another desperate plea for help.

"The Healer from the Unborn Years!" she moaned. "Broichan has imprisoned him in the shrine. I must save him, and I must save Kenneth. What shall I do? Oh, what shall I do?" She tried to push past Aidan but he blocked her way, deaf to her pleas and entreaties to move.

It was when the muffled cry for help came a third time that Aidan suddenly groaned and shook his head violently from side to side, as though trying to free it from some web or snare.

"I am coming, my blood-brother," he whispered. "I am coming!" His voice rose to a triumphant shout. Springing from the rock, he seized one of the stones which had fallen from the burning shrine and hurled it at the boar as it prepared to charge Kenneth again.

"To your feet, my brave boy!" he shouted, and now he was a man transformed, exulting at the prospect of danger and fighting. "Set my blood-brother free while I rid us of this beast."

Recognizing the old, confident voice, Kenneth laughed joyfully, and, forgetting his own injury, kicked at the door of the shrine until it burst open.

"To your feet, Drust. I need your help now more than ever I did," Aidan shouted, stepping aside as the boar charged.

"I obey, my prince." Unsteadily Drust pulled himself out of the mud and swayed a little, waiting for the pain to subside.

"Shall I finish him off now so that we may make a meal of him for supper?" the prince asked, helping himself to Drust's dagger and at the same time watching the figure that Kenneth was helping from the burning shrine. Yes, it was John, the Healer, John his blood-brother.

"This creature is the Great White One," Drust muttered, watching as the boar turned from one side to another, undecided which enemy to attack. "Do not forget that he is your god. If you kill him, what will your people say? What will happen to them? Only a god can kill a god, or someone who does not believe that the Great White One is a god at all. Let me dispatch him, my prince."

"You are no match for the Great White One now, my brave Drust," Aidan answered, but Bridie could detect the uneasiness in his tone as he suddenly grasped the choice of action forced on him. It was so simple —their lives, or that of his god. And to slay the god would mean deliberately flouting one of the oldest and most powerful of their religious prohibitions: unless he withdrew immediately into voluntary exile, he would bring misfortune not only on himself, but on all his people.

Overhead the thunder cracked, and this time the accompanying lightning was followed by a violent tremor and the rumbling of falling rocks. Sensing that his victims were distracted the boar picked up Drust's blood scent and had twisted his head for a final charge when —above the howl of the gale, the roaring of the burning trees, the crash of tumbling rocks—there came the high screams of his panic-stricken herd, fleeing downhill from the rapidly advancing fire.

"Help my blood-brother to the rock," Aidan shouted to Kenneth. "Come, Drust, my most faithful friend." And he half-led, half-carried the dwarf away from the sanctuary and the sightless beast that waited there in silence.

"It is a nightmare without any end," John said, but as he spoke he was pulling off his shirt and tearing it into strips to bind up the wound in Kenneth's arm.

And then the first of the herd appeared.

Choked with smoke, blind with terror they surged out of the wood, squealing and grunting. If one faltered, those behind trampled it into the soft earth. They blundered into young saplings, snapping them off at their roots with the weight of their numbers; they charged the great, unyielding oaks, and died among the acorns that might have been their food. Through the raging furnace of the shrine they poured, bringing down the last of the walls; across the sanctuary they hurled themselves, oblivious in their terror of the Great White One standing there. Loudly the huge beast squealed in one last desperate attempt to assert his authority over those he had mated and sired, had fought and beaten.

On the rock the silent group watched as the terror-stricken herd raced towards their leader, faltered a moment, engulfed him and thundered on, to be lost among the trees below.

Shuddering, Bridie closed her eyes. Inside of her was a strange feeling, which she knew could only be pity, for the end of the boar. She could not understand herself.

"So the Great White One perished under the feet of his own kind," Aidan said slowly.

"Would you have killed him?" Drust asked, spitting on his hands and rubbing the saliva on such of his injuries as he could reach.

"How can I tell? When a man is fighting for his life, or the life of a friend. . . ." He shrugged his shoulders. "It was a decision I did not have to make, and for that I am thankful. But we must get away from here and out of the Forest as quickly as possible. The herd will have cleared a path for us that we can follow."

As they climbed down the rock—victors not victims—and hurried away, it seemed to Bridie that never, as long as she lived, would she forget the roaring and crackling of the fires behind them as they devoured the terrifying wooden statues, destroying for ever all that they and the Great White One had symbolized.

# 8 The Hooded Ones

THEY FLUNG themselves down, exhausted, by the banks of a shallow burn, and scooping up the soft, peaty water in their hands they splashed it over their faces, bathed their wounds and rinsed out their mouths, trying to remove the taste of smoke and fear and death, while away to the north-west the fire raged through the Especially Sacred Forest.

Bridie sat apart, lost in troubled thoughts. No one had paid any attention to her since they had fled from the Rock of the Victims: no one had thanked her for bringing down the fire which had saved their lives; but for once she was glad to be ignored. Some new, terrible magic had possessed her when she called on the great forces of nature to obey her and at that moment she knew she was indeed the daughter of a goddess and a goddess herself. This knowledge had served to carry her through the ensuing events, but now that the danger from the Great White One was over, she realized the terrible drain on her strength. Her hands shook, her legs could not support her, her body was hollow, and long, agonizing shudders racked it again and again.

How could she continue, day after day, year after year—as did her mother—to answer the prayers of her people when so much was demanded of her thoughts and her body?

Before she could resolve her problem, Aidan sprang to his feet, impatient for action.

"Drust, my friend, are you well enough to accompany me to Dunadd? I know whom my warriors will support in any struggle for power between their king and his chief priest, but I must warn them at once of Broichan's treachery."

"Take the bandage off your left hand," Drust said, and Bridie, immediately forgetting about herself, turned away so that she should not see the horror and disbelief on the prince's face as memory returned.

"How did I forget?" he whispered.

"That was Broichan's work," Drust answered, and Bridie saw now how he fought to conceal the pain that stabbed him every time he spoke or drew a deep breath.

"I knew this once, and then I forgot," Aidan said slowly, his anger mounting as he realized the significance of what had happened in the

Forest of the Great White One. "I was to die in there!" he shouted. "Broichan meant to bring out my blood-brother, John, to reign in my place." His face distorted, he stooped over John, his clutching fingers closing round his neck.

"We understand one another's words, but are woefully ignorant of events," John said quietly, and he drew Aidan's left hand down and began to rebandage it with great care. "Why was I imprisoned for days in that foul hut?" he asked, keeping his voice low and calm. "Why did a voice in my heavy sleep keep on telling me I was a prince and soon I would be a king?"

"My blood-brother," Aidan whispered, the hatred dying as swiftly as it had surged up. "We loved each other once. Why are we strangers now?"

"Because I am a stranger to myself," John answered. "Broichan found selfishness and ambition in me that I did not know I possessed. I am ashamed."

"Your shame must wait its turn," Drust said impatiently. "Broichan will have his priests out to discover what has caused the fire in the Especially Sacred Forest. We must be away from Dalriada before he finds out. We should have until dawn, but—"

Breaking off, he gestured to the others to remain silent and bending down so that his ear was just above the running burn, he listened intently and then straightened up.

"Surely the daughter of the High One can hear it now?" he asked mockingly. Whatever pain he now suffered was under his iron control.

"Yes, I can hear it now," Bridie answered. "It is the Washer at the Ford, the Hag who controls our destinies, and now she is playing the Remembering Strain."

Such light as there was from the burning forest was obscured by the smoke and drifting mist so that she could not see the singer, but the song was soft and nostalgic, the chords rippled and fell like the splash of a waterfall on a drowsy summer's day, and memory, erratic and distorted at first, began to creep back.

Kenneth moaned as the music and his throbbing wound took him out of the world of Dalriada, erased all memory of its ancient language, and he was a schoolboy again.

"John, my arm hurts so much. And I'm frightened. Can't we go home now, to Mum and Dad and Sheena?"

"Of course we can." Nothing in his voice betrayed his relief and exultation that his young brother had returned to him. "Don't you worry. I'll take you back." He looked at Aidan, who turned to Drust.

"Broichan brought you here," the dwarf pointed out. "It would appear that he brought Kenneth too, from the strange tongue he now speaks. But of this you can be sure—he will not waste time and energy helping you to go back when he can get rid of you in a much easier fashion."

"Perhaps there is something I can do," Bridie said, after a moment's hesitation. She knew now that she was suffering from a growing loss of identity which had begun some time back with the weakening of her senses of hearing and smell, but the harp music, which appeared to have confused the Healer and Kenneth, had suddenly increased her confidence—not in herself, but in her mother, and for the first time suspicion grew within her that the fire which had saved them was perhaps not her work at all, but that of the goddess. "At least let me try to help you," she begged, and before anyone could answer she was on her feet, her face turned to the darkness above, both arms raised in supplication.

"O High One, Great Brigid, goddess of the rushing rivers, the high mountains, the forests and the green plains, most beautiful and radiant of all women—forgive the pride and foolishness of your daughter and help her now."

The harp music grew louder.

Memory stirred. For Bridie it was too frail and elusive to be caught, but Kenneth remembered.

"John, she's Bridie! Our Bridie. She has to go back to Mull with us too. Don't you remember, Bridie? You came from England and stayed with us in Oban because. . . . "

The singing increased. And the music of the harp.

They all saw her. Grey hair now hiding, now revealing the wrinkled, hideous face, grey garments shrouding the shapeless body, the repulsive limbs.

"Do you remember me?" she asked, and saliva dripped from the corner of her mouth.

"I remember you," Bridie answered. She spoke like a child repeating something she had got by heart and did not fully understand. "I met you three times in the Unborn Years. You and Drust and Broichan wanted John, the Healer.

"But my magic was equal to yours. I saved him at Dunadd and I protected Kenneth too. The beadbonny ash protected both Sheena and me outside the cottage. But there was nothing I could do at the old ford once you offered us our hearts' desires."

"It was a renowned physician I wanted to be," John muttered. "Not a king."

"I kept on changing my mind," Kenneth confessed, "and the past always seemed more exciting than the present."

"I dare not admit what I wanted then," Bridie said, "but it has not brought me the happiness I expected."

"So what is it you want now, child?"

"My mother, the High One." The words came tumbling out. "I want her to heal our wounds and bruises, and send the Healer and Kenneth back to their own time. I want her to restore Aidan's fingers so he can be king, and heal Drust's injuries and make him tall and straight and handsome."

"And for yourself?"

"I have not thought about myself yet."

"You believe your mother can do all this?"

"I know she can."

In the wind the Hag's grey hair swirled and twisted, reaching out like tentacles to mingle with the thickening mist and isolate the two of them from the others, and Bridie, gazing into the cold, grey eyes, suddenly knew the truth. This repulsive old woman, the Washer at the Ford, was also the High One, her mother.

She wanted to cry out in horror, to turn and run away, but something prevented her, and she stood there, returning the ice-cold look.

"Can you grant my requests, Mother?"

"I can. But why should I, Daughter?"

Bridie looked around her, as though the words she sought might be found on the mists which enclosed them.

"Because no matter what John, the Healer, and Kenneth think, it was I who brought them here. Please help me to take them back."

"If I grant your requests, what in turn will you do for me?"

"Anything you want, Mother."

"Will you live with me until you grow ancient and wrinkled and grey, as I am now? Will you love me throughout the years and the hundreds of years, as a daughter should love her mother?"

Terror and revulsion filled Bridie as she looked at the ugly face; despair overwhelmed her at the thought of living in this alien, pagan world for ever.

"My people will worship you and adore you, as they do me," the Hag continued. "No matter how old or ugly or cruel you grow, to them you will be forever young and beautiful and merciful. Only when they hate or fear you, as you now hate and fear me, will they see you as now you see me."

Stay here? Never return to her own world, to the love and warmth of her own family? Family? She had none. No, that was not true, and the time was coming when she must face the truth. Not now. Soon. Friends? Yes, it was safe to think about friends.

"If you will send John, the Healer, and Kenneth back, I will stay with you and love you," she answered steadily. "But I do not want your people to worship me or think I am what I now know I am not."

"That is your decision?"

"Yes—Mother."

"Look at me, child," the goddess commanded, and again Bridie met the chill, inhuman gaze. "I see only sacrifice and resignation, Brigid. I can find no love in you." She turned away, but not before Bridie had seen the loneliness that clouded the clear eyes.

"Give me time," she pleaded. "Give me time, Mother. I am full of love, but I have wasted it on dreams and make-believe. I have seen only the surface of people. Give me time, Mother, for I feel a new love burning within me already." Flinging her arms round the Hag, she kissed her on the brow and cheek, and then on the sad, wrinkled mouth. "You are my mother, and because I love you and need you just as you need me, I shall stay here with you."

The wind tugged and teased at the mists, so that they thinned out and Bridie could see the others staring at the goddess. Dazed, she stepped back from the shining woman, more beautiful than anyone she had ever seen before. Memory stirred. Had there not been someone equally beautiful in the Unborn Years? Beautiful when loved and loving, ugly when hated and hating? No, it was no use. She couldn't remember, couldn't think properly. All she could do was stare at the goddess, watching how the light from the burning forest was reflected in the gems and gold embroidery on her dress, the jewels in her corn-gold hair, the rings on her arms and fingers.

Only Aidan and Drust, wise in the ways of their deities, remained unmoved, accepting the change in the Hag just as they had accepted the change in Kenneth and Bridie.

"My daughter would trade her life for yours," the goddess said softly —and again, for a moment, it seemed to Bridie she had heard that voice in the Unborn Years—"but the time when I might have accepted such a sacrifice has long since gone. We have had our day, we gods of the Celtic peoples.

"Already many who once worshipped me have turned to a new God, called Jesus. Already a new goddess, the servant of Mary, the mother of this Jesus, has taken my name and does my work, and she will remain in the hearts of women as Saint Brigid when I am only a fragment in the dream of some yet unborn Celtic poet.

"But I am still the High One, with powers that are more than mortal. My daughter has told me what she wants for each of you. Is her desire yours?"

"I feel so ill," Kenneth whispered. "I want to go home, please."

Aidan stepped forward and bowed low before the goddess. "I beg of you, O High One, to send back to their own time my blood-brother, my foster-brother, and your own daughter."

"And you, O prince?"

"It would be best for Drust and me to leave Dalriada for Ireland and ask there for help to break the power of Broichan."

"Escape with my help, Aidan?" the goddess asked, with an ironic smile. "And in return what will you do? Listen to the teaching of the priest, Columba; ally yourself with the Northern Picts who already worship this new God, Jesus, so that one day Columba, not Broichan, will crown you on the rock of Dunadd—and I shall be discarded along with the Great White One?"

Aidan had no answer to make, but Drust laughed out loud. "Why not, O High One? You yourself have admitted your day is over. This new God does not demand physical perfection in his kings. As you say, Columba will accept Aidan and crown him king, and there will be peace between Dalriada and the North—for a time, at any rate."

"And you, my cynical friend? Are you too prepared to accept favours from me before you prostrate yourself in front of Columba?"

"If you will forgive blunt speaking, High One, Columba and his God mean no more to me than did the Great White One—or you, yourself. My gods, like the race from which I am sprung, are older than any of you: they have served me well in the past and I propose to allow them to serve me well in the future.

"I ask no favours from you. I am capable of leaving Dalriada without your help. As for this body which concerns your daughter, assure her that I have lived so long with it that I understand it and it understands me. Such friends as I have know it is the mind and spirit of Man which matter, and not the body which contains them.

"Your daughter meant well, but she must learn that she cannot change people to please herself—in Dalriada or elsewhere." He swayed, and would have fallen had Aidan not steadied him.

"Your body is your own affair, Drust, but the injuries it has suffered are mine," the prince observed. "You were proposing to swim to Ireland? Forget your pride and accept the help of the High One to leave Dalriada."

This time the dwarf did not argue, but Bridie, seeing the grey pallor of his face as he turned aside, suddenly understood how Drust's gods were to serve him, and could have wept with sorrow.

With a sign to them to be still, the goddess knelt by the banks of the burn and stared into the dark moving water, her breathing growing more and more laboured until she cried out, as though she could endure no more, and then after a pause she rose slowly to her feet.

"Broichan is in the Hall of Dunadd, trying to rouse the men who have feasted and drunk all night. He knows that the shrine and the Great White One have perished in the fire which still rages through the Especially Sacred Forest. He is sending scouts and messengers—anyone who can stand upright—to find out what has happened to the prince and the Healer. He is berating Domnull of the Hundred Battles for leaving the Fort of the Seagulls in the charge of his wife—forgetting that Domnull survived half his battles because his wife fought by his side.

"Soon Broichan will send his mind abroad, as I sent mine, and he will see that he has five people to fear, not two. You must be far from Dalriada before that. The Fort of the Seagulls. We can reach it before Domnull, and you can take one of the boats beached in the bay below.

"Let us go now. Aidan, carry my harp, and when we come to the Great Moss, throw it as far away from you as possible so that it may sink to the bottomless depths. I shall play it no more, and it is not fitting that any other hands should touch it."

With the goddess leading the way, they set off through drifting mist and darkness. Every now and again Kenneth stifled a moan of pain, until finally he staggered and fell to his knees.

"You're all right, laddie," John said. "Lift him on to my back, Aidan, will you? That's it. Now, arms round my neck, Kenneth. All right. The good arm round my neck." And they were off again.

When they reached the edge of the Great Moss the goddess hurried on ahead, unable to bear the sound of the bog waters closing over the magic strings of her harp, and lapping greedily round the frame fashioned from pinewood and carved with strange, interlacing, birdheaded animals, inlaid with gold and decorated with jet and precious stones.

Drust stumbled next and Aidan reached quickly to save him, wincing at the involuntary use of his left hand.

"Shall we throw dice to find out who carries whom?" Drust asked wryly. "Or perhaps the daughter of the goddess will carry us both?"

Tired, bruised and hungry, torn between two worlds and uncertain to which she belonged, Bridie listened to the dwarf's laboured breathing and realized that already the old gods were calling him home to rest, but that not until his prince was safe would he heed their call.

"Let us hope that the wife of Domnull of the Hundred Battles sleeps as soundly at night as she fights on the field of battle," Aidan said as they skirted the base of the fort and began to scramble down the cliff, with the thunder of sea music to spur them on.

Now, in the pallid light of early dawn, they could see the long sea boats, seal skins stretched tautly over wooden frames, drawn up alongside one another in the little bay.

They saw too the group of figures in cowled cloaks standing, silent and menacing, between them and the boats.

"I have had enough, and more than enough, of fighting today," Aidan said, reaching for Kenneth's dagger with a sigh.

"I am glad of that, Aidan, prince of Dalriada," the tallest of the cowled figures answered, stepping forward with his hands clasped in front of him, "for we are men of peace." Without waiting for a reply he threw back his hood and turned to the goddess.

"I salute you, great Brigid, the High One."

"And I salute you, Columba, prince and priest."

"I offer greetings to one who is older by far than my people, and three who have come from the Unborn Years—and would return there."

"How do you know about us?" John asked, putting down the now sleeping Kenneth and trying to hide his anxiety.

Columba smiled reassuringly.

"News travels faster by word of mouth than by any means known in the Unborn Years, my son. High One, can you send them back to that time from which your magic and Broichan's summoned them?"

"Only with your help, Columba. Here in Dalriada I can already feel Broichan working against me. Take us in your sea-boats out into the ocean and there I shall use my powers for the last time to undo what has been done."

"You do not need to bargain with me to get my help, great Brigid."

"I know that, Columba, but I know too that the time has come to leave my people to you and the hooded ones, and to join the heroes and heroines of old in Tir-nan-Og, the Land of Happiness, where there is no sadness or unhappiness, envy or pride, hate or jealousy, decay or death."

Columba bowed his head and then turned to one of his men.

"What are our prospects if we cross to Ireland now, brother?"

"I do not like the feel of the changing wind, or the smell of the thickening fog, Columba. There will be a storm within the hour, and one it were better to avoid."

"As we cannot do that, we must put our trust in God." There was only the slightest hesitation before he continued, "and in Brigid, the High One."

"Your God chose wisely when he sent you, Colomba, a prince and courtier, to convert my people," the goddess acknowledged.

With only the faintest sigh Drust collapsed at the feet of his prince, and when Aidan knelt beside him, speaking his name softly, there was no reply, no movement.

One of the cowled figures raised his hand and began to make the sign of the cross but stopped at a glance from Columba.

Hot tears welled up in Bridie's eyes as she watched how tenderly Aidan lifted the lifeless body of the dwarf and placed it in the boat, and she wished—now that it was too late—she had been able to say how sorry she was for misjudging him, how foolish she had been not to realize it was the man and not the shell that mattered.

When one of the hooded figures led her away from the others she offered no protest, and it was only when a dirty hand was clamped over her mouth so that she had no chance to cry out that she realized this was not one of Columba's men.

"Where is she?" a harsh voice whispered. "Where is my princess? Tell me at once if you value your life."

"What princess?" Bridie asked as the hand was eased a little. "I don't know what you're talking about."

"Child! Where are you? We are ready to leave." Again the hand clamped over her mouth as the goddess called through the mists and gloom.

"She is in this boat," the man holding Bridie shouted. "She is worn out and sleeps."

Desperately Bridie tried to free herself from the iron strength of the hands, conscious that the creaking of the oars and the sound of voices were dying away in the noise of the wind and the crash of the waves against the foot of the cliffs on both sides of the bay.

"My princess! Where is she?" The hands seized her shoulders and shook her until she cried out in terror. They had gone—everyone she knew, and she was left in Dalriada at the mercy of this madman and Broichan, in an age of cruelty and fear.

The cowl fell back from the man's face so that she saw his features for the first time.

"Calum!" she whispered incredulously. Surely the old fisherman belonged to Mull and the other life to which she could never now return.

"Aye, it's Calum. Now, answer me. Where is Sheena? What have you done with her, you meddling English witch?"

"Calum! I don't understand you. I. . . . "

"Where is Sheena?" His hands closed on her shoulders again.

"No, no, Don't hurt me, Calum. Sheena didn't come with us. Only John and Kenneth. Ask them, if you don't believe me. Shout out and ask them."

"Sheena was with you at the old ford when the Hag and the pries[t] brought you back here. She was crying for help, and me too drunk t[o] hear."

"Yes, she was at the ford, but she didn't come with us. I haven't see[n] her. I swear I haven't. Perhaps the beadbonny ash protected her."

"My princess cried for help not three hours past. Think, Brigid o[f] Barra. Think!" His voice was less fierce now, as though he realized that terrifying her would only prevent her concentrating.

His princess? Bridie's hand crept up to her mouth and she gnawed at her thumb in fear as she remembered the soft voice saying, 'It was Drust who comforted me, once the daughter of a king, and helped me to bear the lot of a slave'.

"Danu," she whispered. "Sheena was Danu, and I never recognized her. Danu—my slave."

Calum winced.

"Where is she now?"

She could tell how hard he was fighting to control himself.

"I sent her back to her own people—the Northern Picts."

"Attended?"

"Alone. There was no one to send. But I didn't know it was Sheena. Kenneth didn't either. He talked to her and went to her for comfort, but he had no idea she was Sheena. But then he didn't know he was Kenneth either—the Kenneth of Oban and Mull, I mean."

"Where is she now?"

Bridie began to cry.

"I don't know, Calum. How can I possibly know?"

"Stop crying and listen to me." The old man's voice was as hard as the volcanic rock of his island. "In your selfishness and ignorance you are meddling in the old arts, and now it is disaster you are bringing, not only on yourself, but on the gentle one who loved you, as she loved the little sister who died.

"There is still the magic about you, you that was once the daughter of the High One. You can help me save my princess. Look into the mists and tell me where she is. Think only of Danu . . . Danu . . . Danu. . . ."

The roaring of the wind, the crash and surge of the wild waves, faded: there was wind-whipped water—fresh water—a dwelling of stone as befitted the daughter of a goddess—a causeway on stilts. . . .

"She has gone back to our home in the middle of the Loch of the Ash Tree." But she dared not tell him that the rowan lay dead among the reeds.

"Good girl."

Now he had no words to spare, but whether this was because he was till angry or because he was old and wanted to conserve his energy, she had no means of knowing.

He helped her up the cliff to where two shaggy hill-ponies were waiting, indicated to her to remove her own green cloak and put on the dark habit of the followers of the new God, and then they set off for the dwelling she had hoped never to see again.

Smoke eddied from the still burning forest and wild animals—wolves, deer, foxes, cats, and once a bear with its cub—crossed their path, fleeing blindly from the oldest enemy of all. To the soldiers or peasants they passed, they were men of Columba's faith, to be greeted with scorn or respect according to the individual's belief, but to be allowed to travel freely through Dalriada until Broichan decreed otherwise.

Calum was well ahead when they approached the lake dwelling, and when, incredibly weary and stiff, Bridie dismounted by the edge of the loch, it was to watch Calum carrying Sheena across the causeway, talking to her in the soft voice a mother might use to reassure a frightened child, while Sheena clung to him, eyes wide with terror. She did not appear to recognize Bridie and neither then, nor in all the long journey when Calum's pony carried a double load, did she attempt to speak.

Bridie ached in every limb and she was so tired that her eyes smarted with the effort to keep them open. Once or twice she fell into a light doze, awakening with a shock to find herself half-way out of the saddle. She wanted to call out that she was too exhausted to go any farther, but she knew she must not add to Calum's worry. Sheena, his princess, came first with him, she knew, but she was also sure that, no matter what he might have said, he would never ride on and abandon her. If she could not keep up the killing pace, they would all be captured and taken to Broichan. And then. . . ?

When they came to steep rocks and heather and low berry-bearing bushes, they dismounted, and Calum turned the horses loose to find their own way back to wherever it was he had stolen them.

From there, they continued on foot, climbing, slipping, pulling themselved up by tufts of coarse grass, gasping for breath, until they reached great slabs of flat rock, and then, without a pause they began the steep climb down, with the hungry roar of the sea growing ever more deafening, and the gale trying to prise loose chilled fingers from their precarious grasp in cracks and crevices.

Bridie shrieked in terror as a great black and white bird, its long pointed orange beak aimed at her eyes, swooped down on her repeatedly. But there was no one to help or protect her. Calum was concerned only with Sheena, and not until they reached the foot of the cliff, where the sea snarled among the jagged rocks, did the bird stop attacking her.

She recognized the small wooden rowing boat at once as the one Calum used on Loch Scridain, and her heart sank as she looked beyond, where the waves crashed and retreated and crashed forward again. Even if they could survive the long sea voyage to Mull in that frail craft, how could they return to their own time? She could do nothing to help. Her magic—if ever there had been any magic—had gone now. She was only a frightened child, looking to the adult world for help.

Calum touched her shoulder briefly.

"There is no need for worrying. I am coming through the years for you, and I am taking you back again with me." And he helped them into the boat, grasped the oars which he himself had made when he was young and foolhardy and boastful, and began to row with the current, heading gradually out into the open sea, the boat now rising with the white-crested breakers, now falling smoothly into the grey trough, while overhead the seabirds screamed and mewed.

There was no break in the rhythm of his rowing when Bridie called out in fright and pointed to the headland they had just left, to the figure that stood there, arms outstretched, robes and head-dress billowing in the wind: where the towering cliff would have dwarfed an ordinary man, now it added to the stature and authority of Broichan, high priest of Dalriada.

Above the howling of the wind and the roar of the breakers there came a new sound, a high-pitched, eerie whistling. Calum's mouth tightened.

"He is summoning up a west wind," Bridie shouted.

"That wind will come without any summoning from Broichan," Calum grunted.

With a sweep of his hand the figure on the headland dismissed the hesitant sun and the clouds closed over it, while at the same time the rain began to fall again, cold and remorseless, pitting the angry sea, obscuring the gesticulating figure, blotting out the black skerries and islands; and as the wind began to change it seemed to Bridie that they were the only people in the world—Calum and Sheena and herself —and this world consisted entirely of a grey ocean which would inevitably claim them as its own.

Doggedly Calum bent over his oars, pulled and straightened up, bent, pulled and straightened. Once the wild winds bore snatches of a low, mournful singing, like that of some doomed, enchanted people, and then as they drew nearer Bridie caught a glimpse of a group of seals huddled together on a lonely skerry, and she could feel their sad eyes following them until the mist and the rain swallowed them up.

Faster and stronger the sea ran now and Calum's face, grim and expressionless, might have been carved from wood. As he swung the stern of the boat into a massive breaker, Bridie clutched Sheena to her as though to protect her, shivering as the bow rose under the rushing roaring wave before plunging into the trough, to be positioned for the next breaker. But no man, she knew—not even Calum—could fight this storm single-handed for much longer.

The roar and noise increased as fresh waves swept against the side of the boat and broke into it, while ahead, breakers coming from different directions met head-on, rearing up into tremendous waterfalls and spilling out into vast whirlpools which spread greedily towards the tired fisherman and his battered, sinking craft.

Now the boat began to spin round, slowly at first and then faster and faster, and the broken waters reached out to close over it.

It was Sheena the waves claimed first, snatching her greedily from Bridie's arms. Calum leaped after her immediately, shouting out something to Bridie, but his words were lost in the terrible noise and turmoil. A few moments later, when the seas swept her from the sinking craft, she closed her eyes wearily, making no attempt to swim or save herself.

"Child!"

Recognizing the voice, she forced open her eyes but could see no one.

"High One?" she whispered.

"Katie!" It was the same voice.

"Mummy!" she cried out in anguish, knowing now that tthe High One—so beautiful when loved and loving—was also her own mother, Jennifer Nicholson; and with this knowledge the last remnants of her old hatred and envy and unhappiness were washed away by the waves, leaving only a great love and the beginning of understanding.

"Listen to me, Katie, even though you can't see me. You are quite safe. Calum and his People of the Sea are caring for you, but my love, however imperfect it might have been, is a greater protection than their magic."

"Oh, Mummy," Bridie cried. "I'm sorry. I'm so sorry. I've loved you all the time. I always will love you, no matter what you say or do."

"I know, child. I understand, Katie. Sleep now. I shall look after you and love you as I always have done—in my own way."

And as the cold plunging waves cradled her in their embrace, Bridie closed her eyes again and slept.

# 9  Dream of Dalriada

"SHE IS really beautiful," Sheena said.

Bridie smiled in agreement. People who didn't know talked about clever photographers, or skilful make-up, or special stage-lighting, but Bridie knew that none of these really mattered. It was Jennifer Nicholson herself who mattered. She was really beautiful. And growing older made no difference, except, perhaps, to add to that beauty.

In a companionable silence the two girls looked down through one of the splayed windows of McCaig's Tower, watching as the yachts with their coloured sails drifted across the splendid blue of the sea below.

"And she loves you very much," Sheena continued.

Again Bridie smiled. Everyone knew how her mother had handed her part over to her understudy within an hour of hearing of this second accident to her daughter. Martin had arranged for a private plane to fly them from London to Mull and had even brought up the psychiatrist in whose care Bridie had been previously. They had wanted to move Bridie to a nursing home on the mainland, or to bring over a nurse from there, but Jennifer had said no. Katie was all she had now. She would nurse her herself. Gently but firmly she refused all offers of help from the Mac-Donalds. Perhaps there wasn't much she could do, but at least she could sit by her child's bedside, could be there when Katie returned from her strange dream world.

A bed was put up in Bridie's room, and Jenny slept there, wakening immediately whenever Bridie moved, to murmur soothing, loving endearments.

"She was very upset when you told her you wanted to come back to Oban with us. I think she's afraid you won't ever go back to her. I don't think you understand just how much you mean to her."

Bridie reached out and stroked the back of Sheena's hand with one finger.

"Oh, yes, I do. I do. That's why I'm well now—just because I understand so much about her that I didn't understand before. All you know about her is what you've seen here, and because you have the kind of mother who doesn't change, you think Jenny must be like that. But she isn't.

"Your mother loves your father and all three of you all the time.

"But what Jenny really loves is the idea of herself in the role of the loving mother. And that's exactly what it is, a role, and she just can't keep it up, month after month, year after year.

"You see, it was Daddy she loved. And it was Jenny that Daddy loved, not those dolly-girls he used to take out.

"They quarrelled terribly, Jenny and Daddy, because they were so alike. It didn't matter where they were or who they were with. It was worst for me when they had rows at home, especially when I was little. I couldn't bear to hear them shouting at each other, or listen to the terrible things they said. You see, I loved them both, and thought they were both wonderful.

"And then quite suddenly they'd make it up—whatever 'it' was—and they'd ring up a baby-sitter, or dump me on one of the neighbours, and go off and celebrate, and forget all about me; and next day Jenny'd have a great bunch of flowers or some fantastic brooch or bracelet or a new dress or something.

"When I got older, they tried to get me to take sides. I didn't want to. But in the end—well—I chose Daddy. The doctor said it was quite normal at my age to think my father was marvellous.

"And he really was marvellous, Sheena. Good-looking—and clever with people, so he got what he wanted without them knowing it.

"I suppose in a way I loved him because I was sorry for him. He was afraid of the future. All he could play was lean, handsome, young men, and he kept on asking me what he'd do when people found out he wasn't handsome or young any longer.

"Of course I was jealous of Jenny because she was beautiful and everyone fell in love with her. I'm plain and dumpy, and no one ever fell in love with me. Perhaps no one ever will. It didn't help when Jenny kept finding fault with me for being clumsy and stupid. I suppose she was disappointed in me. I wasn't the kind of daughter she wanted, and not all the model clothes or expensive schools could alter me.

"She couldn't bear to look at me after the crash on the Motorway. That's when I really knew how much and how long I'd hated her. All she could think of was Daddy. She screamed at me, saying I was old enough to know when he'd been drinking. I should never have gone out with him so late at night. She said that it was my fault he was dead.

"She didn't really mean it. She was hysterical.

"But in a way, it was true.

"It was all made easier for her. She had Martin to look after her. And she went back to that Ibsen play the day after the funeral. Everyone said how courageous she was, how she'd added a new dimension to her performance.

"But I had no one, Sheena. I was so unhappy I just wanted to die. I hated Jenny and I hated myself for hating her. There was nothing for me in the present or the future, and gradually I slipped back into the past—a past that had never existed. It was so easy. I just imagined the kind of father I'd always wanted, and made up all kinds of impossible adventures for us, and shut everyone else out. That way, I could go on living.

"When people noticed and told Jenny and she started to worry and to love me again, it was too late. I knew I couldn't depend on her any more. I stopped hating her, because as far as I was concerned, she didn't exist. There was just me and Daddy."

She fell silent.

Beyond Kerrera, the hills of Mull were clear cut against the cloudless sky. Trailing a white, ever-widening wake, a steamer made its dignified way past Lady's Rock.

"People make mistakes," Sheena said gently. "And mothers are people, you know."   "Yes, I know. I understand that now. Having that strange—" She hesitated, looking at Sheena for the right word.

"Daddy calls it your dream of Dalriada," Sheena reminded her, and this time Bridie laughed at this easy acceptance of something she still found inexplicable.

"Yes. Having that strange dream has helped me to understand so many things about her. I know that Jenny will go on making the same mistakes all her life. If I'm ill again, she'll drop everything and fly to help me. Once I'm better, once she's given her ideal mother performance —one that's good enough to satisfy herself and her public—then she'll return to the stage, or perhaps she'll 'rest' a few months and be the ideal wife to Martin. She'll adore him, especially when she remembers how rich and successful and Big Business he is. She won't quarrel with him, because Martin isn't the quarrelling type. She'll miss that. She enjoyed those quarrels, although she'd never admit it. It'll probably be a very good marriage . . . for her."

"You don't like Martin, then?"

"I didn't say that. It's just that he wants Jenny and I'm included in the package deal, whether he likes it or not."

"I think he does like it, Bridie. He talked about you a great deal when you were ill, and he kept on asking us about you—what you liked to read, to do . . . that kind of thing."

"Oh, yes, I think he quite likes me," Bridie agreed, and the flush of colour in her cheeks showed how pleased she was to have Sheena confirm this. "But Jenny will make sure that he is *her* husband and not *my* stepfather.

"People think that all women want children, and when they've got them, love them. I've learned that this isn't true. Jenny wants fame, money and an adoring husband. She tries to want me, but it's the only role she can't keep up. It's not her fault. The doctor said there are lots of career women like her. And some without careers too. You haven't got to like children because you're a woman.

"I understand now that I can't change her. I must accept what love she can offer, when she feels like offering it, and I must look after myself when she forgets about me, or hasn't time for me. It won't be so hard now that I've stopped thinking and behaving like a child."

Again she fell silent. Behind them, on the grass in the centre of the Tower, a group of little children in the care of an older girl were singing lustily, in several different keys and a variety of tunes—

I'll do all that ever I can
To follow the gaberlunzie-man

and falling about in an ecstasy of delight as each in turn pretended to be the gypsy, and tried to imitate the playing and the sound of some musical instrument.

Compared with them, Bridie thought, she was completely adult, though she had to admit, if only to herself, that there were times when she felt as childish and vulnerable as the youngest boy, who had just tripped over a stone and was crying loudly for sympathy.

"Of course your family helped me more than you'll ever know, Sheena. I'd never met anyone like you. You were so nice and kind that I kept on grabbing, trying to make everyone like me."

"Talking into Daddy's tape recorder helped, didn't it?" Sheena asked.

"Oh, yes. That was a marvellous idea."

At first it had been impossible to free herself of the events in that last fantastic world she had created: at times she didn't know who she was. Or where. Each time she fell asleep she was terrified she'd waken up in Dalriada.

She didn't want to talk about it to her mother or Martin or her doctors. They'd never have understood.

She was quite prepared to tell the MacDonalds, in her own way, and in her own time. And that was when Uncle Graham had suggested his tape recorder.

She just talked into it when she felt like it. When she remembered something. Events in the wrong order. She could play it back and cut bits out if she wanted. Aunt Mary asked if she'd like to have it all typed out so that she could read it and rearrange it. Dear Aunt Mary. If only Jenny had been more like. . . . No. She must never think of that again.

How could she dream about things she'd never heard of, Bridie had wondered. But apparently this often happened. She might have been in the room when the MacDonalds were talking about the past, and could have stored away facts without being aware of it.

She could quite easily have glanced at one of John's medical books and seen the illustration of that nineteenth-century blood transfusion when the coachman offered his blood to save the life of the young mother. She'd forgotten about it because it was of no interest at the time, or because she was more interested in something else. It had hidden itself in one of the lumber rooms of her memory, and had been brought out when her dream world needed information.

As for the people—most of them had actually lived at that time, but they had taken on the characteristics of her own relations and friends —not perhaps as they actually were, but as she saw or imagined them.

Naturally she played the chief role, idealized, so that she was older, beautiful and clever—all the things she had secretly wished she was—a perfectly normal occurrence, her uncle assured her, and one not limited to the dreams of childhood or adolescence.

"You know, Sheena, what I just can't understand is how I went fishing with Calum that night. Me—go fishing. I can understand you going out with him. And John and Kenneth. But me! And I still can't remember anything about the very end and how we were rescued."

"That storm came up very suddenly," Sheena reminded her. "The boat John and Kenneth were in was beginning to sink when a student from the Iona Community saw them and rowed out to help. He rescued the two boys and got them safely on to the rocks."

"And then disappeared."

"He told John he didn't want any publicity," Sheena said, trying to sound reasonable. "He returned to the Abbey Guest House and told them what had happened, and while some of the other students went for John and Kenneth, he collected his belongings, took the ferry across to Mull. . . ."

"And disappeared."

"Yes. There could be all kinds of perfectly good reasons why he didn't want people to know where he was or what he was doing." Sheena didn't sound very convinced herself. How could she be convinced when none of the other Iona students knew anything about him or could even recall what he looked like?

"Calum. . . ." Bridie said, very quietly.

"Poor Calum," Sheena whispered, tears springing to her eyes.

Clouds, bluish-grey above, pink below, drifted across the sky: low on the horizon streamers of crimson and dark blue merged into the mists which were beginning to veil the brilliance of the setting sun: crimson light touched the hill tops of Mull and Morvern, transforming them so that they might have been part of some other, magic world—of Tir-nan-Og perhaps, the land of eternal youth and happiness.

Above the joyful shrieks of the children, who were now being pursued by the ghost who lived at the bottom of the garden, Bridie heard someone calling her name, and she turned to see Kenneth running over the grass towards them, one shirt sleeve rolled up to display the spectacular scar on his forearm, his eyes bright with excitement.

Sprawling on the grass, he looked up at his sister.

"Have you told her?"

"Not yet."

"But you've been up here the whole afternoon. What've you been doing?"

"Talking."

"Talking? And you haven't told her?" He gave an exaggerated sigh.

"Told me what?" Bridie asked.

"Well. . . ." Sheena hesitated. "You know that yesterday you gave Kenneth and me one of the copies Mummy typed of your—'dream of Dalriada'?"

"Yes?"

"Of course you'd told us quite a lot about it, but that was the first time we read the whole adventure from the beginning to the end." Both Sheena and her brother were watching Bridie closely now.

"Do you remember, when I was Danu, your giving me a coiled-bronze snake ring, the head set with eyes of green glass, and then telling me that it would keep me safe on my journey back to the north?"

"Yes," Bridie said, but her eyes were wary.

"And later you and Calum rode back to the Loch of the Ash Tree to look for me. Bridie, you forgot to say anything about finding your ring on the ground by the uprooted rowan."

"Did I? I expect I forgot a lot of things. Oh!" Startled, Bridie stepped back, staring from Sheena to Kenneth. "How did you know I found the ring there?"

"Because that was where I dropped it when the Marsh People captured me. I tried to send out a thought message, asking you for help, but I hadn't the gift you had—or the training. But somehow I knew you'd come in the end, and find it, and know I was in danger. And you did, didn't you? You left Calum crossing the causeway to our loch dwelling and you rode straight back to the edge of the Great Moss. I was on the island of dead cotton grass where they'd carried me, and there was black bog all around.

"No—don't say anything yet, Bridie. Please let me go on. They were laughing, the Marsh People—so horrible with their bleached white faces and skeleton hands, their black hair and clothes, and all the time they shook and trembled with fever and palsy, and they glided over the surface of the Great Moss without sinking or even disturbing the thick, black bog.

"They kept on laughing. I was a princess, and fitting bride for their king. But there was too much colour in my cheeks, too much flesh on my limbs. They promised they would touch me with their marsh fever and leave me for seven long days and nights without food or drink on the island of cotton grass, and after that, they said, I would be the kind of bride their king desired.

"Then you came, Bridie, and pleaded with them.

"The daughter of a goddess, and one who had already escaped from them, was a better bride than a princess, you said.

"I called out to you not to offer yourself, but to go and get help, but you wouldn't listen. One of them lifted me in his revolting, shaking arms and carried me back to where you stood, and they all gibbered and mouthed and danced and snatched at you with their white fingers.

"And that was when Calum came.

"He had carried a twig of the ash tree with three red berries on it. He drew a circle round us with it and thrust the twig in my hand, and told me to keep it, no matter what happened, until I was safely back in the cottage again.

"They screamed and slobbered and moaned—the Marsh People —and grabbed and hooked at the air around us, but they couldn't cross the ash tree's circle of protection. And then Calum talked to them in a language older than your Celtic, Bridie. I could tell that he was bargaining with them, but what he offered I couldn't make out, although I think I know now.

"At last they faded away, their pallid faces sly and gloating, and Calum took us across to the coast and the little bay where his fishing boat was waiting.

"Why did you miss that out, Bridie?" Sheena looked tenderly at the younger girl. "Didn't you want anyone to know you'd offered your life in exchange for mine?"

Bridie stared, thunderstruck.

"How did you know?" she asked, making no attempt to answer Sheena's question. "I never told anyone." How could she explain how ashamed she was that, in her dream, she had made this gentle girl a slave? It was impossible to tell anyone about the Marsh People because it would be as though she were saying, "Look, everyone, I'm not always selfish and bad-tempered". And if no one knew about it, it would be a memory for her to treasure the next time she was unhappy—the thought that she had put someone's life before her own, even if it were only in a dream. "How did you know, Sheena?" she repeated.

"Dear Bridie—because I had the same dream. I don't remember going fishing either, but I do remember the Washer at the Ford, and the whirlwind, and then things are vague until we met outside the gates of Dunadd. After that it's all as you described, except for that bit you missed out"—and Sheena knew, without being told, the reason behind it—"until those holiday-makers found us on the sand at Uisken, on Mull. You had swallowed far more sea-water than I had, and it took you much longer to come round, poor thing. If you don't believe me, Bridie, I can show you the account of my dream I wrote down long before you talked of yours. Or would you like me to describe in detail the design embroidered on my dress? Or on yours?"

"You—you aren't joking?" Bridie looked pathetically from Sheena to Kenneth, and back to Sheena, begging them not to be cruel, not to undermine her still precarious hold on reality.

"No, Bridie, of course I'm not joking. I'm telling you the truth."

"You mean we both had the same dream?"

"Perhaps." Sheena spoke very carefully. "But it's more than that, isn't it, Kenneth?"

"Much more," Kenneth agreed, proud of the way he had kept his promise to say nothing until Sheena said he might. "Much more. Because I had the same dream too. The doctor said this gash on my arm was where I'd scraped it against the rocks, when the student rescued us, but I knew quite well it was where the Great White One gored me when I slipped in the mud in the Especially Sacred Forest."

There was a new alarm in Bridie's eyes now.

"How much do you remember of what happened after I broke up the crowning ceremony at Dunadd?" she asked. "I was pretty—awful—to you, because you had refused to cut the bandage from Aidan's hand."

"Were you?" he asked, with just the right amount of surprise. "No, I don't remember anything about that." That's what Sheena and he had agreed on. Those rocks on the Iona coast had taken more than their fair share of blame for his cuts and bruises, and the doctor had certainly been puzzled by the weals across his back. How he'd hated her for humiliating him in front of the crowd! But he'd got over it. Only Sheena knew, and as far as they were concerned, that incident would never be spoken of again. Bridie wouldn't forget, of course. But then, as Sheena said, everyone made mistakes, and had to live with the memory afterwards. He'd seen Bridie at her imperious worst, just as Sheena had known her at her humble best. If you looked at it the right way, the two incidents sort of cancelled each other out. "No, I don't remember anything about that," he repeated firmly. "All I know is that I think it's pretty odd that the three of us should have had exactly the same dream about exactly the same people in exactly the same time."

From a house nearby, a mother called that tea was ready and the children ran off, shouting:

> Finnan haddies for my tea,
> One for you and two for me,

and everything was very peaceful and very ordinary.

"What about John?" Bridie asked, at length, hoping that that last memory would fade, or would at least teach her to control her temper.

"We don't know," Sheena answered. "If he had the same dream, he doesn't remember a single thing about it."

"Why do we keep on talking about a dream?" Kenneth demanded. "We all know it jolly well wasn't. It really happened."

"But that's impossible," Bridie said, and then added in a hesitating tone, "Isn't it?"

No one answered.

"Well, whatever it was," she continued, "John should know all about it. He was the most important person."

"No." Sheena shook her head. "You were the most important person, Bridie.

"You took us all back to pagan Dalriada. Because we wanted to go, of course. But John—perhaps he was too old, or perhaps there isn't as much of the Celt in him, but he never was anyone except himself. Remember? He always wore his own clothes; he spoke English even after Aidan made him understand Celtic. He always belonged to the twentieth century. Right from the beginning Kenneth and I forgot all about this life. Kenneth was a prince and I was a princess. . . ."

"But you never wanted to be a slave, Sheena?"

Sheena smiled reassuringly.

"I'm far too quiet and negative. I try to be what other people want me to be. You told me you were jealous of me before, and I think it helped you to make me a slave. You're not jealous now, are you?"

"Oh, no, no, no. I love you so much, Sheena. But I'm terribly ashamed."

"O.K.," Kenneth said briskly. "Now forget it, or you'll upset Sheena, and then you'll be more ashamed.

"I think we're beginning to get somewhere at last. We all went back to sixth century Argyll because of you, Bridie."

"But why me? You're the ones who are Scottish. You're the ones who know all about this. . . ." And the sweep of her arm included the lights of Oban, the great land mass of the Western Highlands and the distant Hebrides fading into the Atlantic twilight.

"True," Kenneth agreed. "But it's you who are the great-great-granddaughter of Bridie O'Neill of Barra."

"Calum knew about her," Sheena continued. "He told Daddy that people said she had special gifts which set her apart from other folk. He said some people called her a witch, and others a wise woman —depending on whether she helped them or put a curse on them."

"And special gifts can skip a generation or two," Kenneth added excitedly, "and they sort of pile up until someone gets a really hefty dose. . . .

"Me?"

"You, Bridie," Sheena agreed. "And because you were very unhappy, you were very vulnerable, and Broichan and the High One were able to call you back through the years, and you took us and the one they really wanted—John."

There was a long silence.

"Have you told anyone—Aunt Mary or Uncle Graham or John himself—about this?"

"No." Sheena laughed ruefully. "We don't know if we really believe it ourselves, so how can we expect other people to? Your doctors are quite satisfied that it was all a dream because you've been under such a strain."

"But we're not," Kenneth said stubbornly. "We can't think why we went out in the boats at night, or, if we did, why you and Sheena went with Calum, and John and I went off on our own. And that storm. I don't think it was a student who rescued us and pulled John and me to safety on to the rocks of Iona. I think"—he paused as though gathering himself to withstand ridicule—"I think it was Columba himself. Saint Columba."

"If the old pagan gods could take us back in time, then a Christian saint could help you and John to return to this century," Sheena agreed, and from her smile Kenneth knew she had thought of this long before he had, but whether or not she believed it, he had no means of telling.

"But it was Calum who saved you and me, Sheena," Bridie said.

"If he did, it wasn't the way the newspapers made out," Kenneth announced flatly.

"What do you mean?"

"That business of his boat sinking and him swimming to the Mull shore with Sheena, and then returning for you. I've always known it couldn't have happened that way. Calum couldn't swim a stroke."

"Are you sure?"

"Of course I'm sure. He didn't believe in learning to swim. None of the old fishermen did. Calum said that when your time came and the sea called it was daft to struggle because the sea always won in the end."

"I think I'm beginning to understand now," Bridie said slowly. "At the time I couldn't make out what he said when he argued with the Marsh People. Now I know he offered them himself. With all his knowledge of magic and witchcraft, and all the lore and legend of Mull he was so famous for, he was a far better bargain than a dozen of us—well, a dozen of me, anyway."

She paused, trying to assemble her thoughts. The written account of her dream had ended, for personal reasons, when the seas had swept her from the sinking boat.

"That's it. Calum brought us safely back through the years, Sheena, and then, when he realized he couldn't make the shore, he called on the High One, because she was my mother, and on the People of the Sea." Now she recalled the soft hands which kept her afloat, and the voice of the goddess which was at the same time the voice of Jenny. "He asked them to save us, but he himself. . . ."

"Don't be unhappy for him, Bridie," Sheena begged. "I remember once Daddy asking him why he had never married. He said the sea was his first and only love, and it would be his last one too. I'm sure the People of the Sea knew how terrible it would have been for him if he'd had to return to Dalriada and live for ever with the Marsh People. Once we were safe, the sea claimed him. And he wanted to be claimed—by his first and last and only love."

"She's right, Bridie," Kenneth said, looking very wise. "And I'm glad for him that it happened this way. But I can't help wondering what he'd think of all the fuss that's being made of him now. You know, everyone going round telling everyone else things he's supposed to have said and done—people who hardly knew him. Another couple of years and he'll be a folk hero and there'll be bearded blokes with tape recorders collecting stories about him for the telly or a new book."

Again there was a long silence.

From her pocket Sheena drew a withered twig, toyed with it and then, seeing the questioning look in Bridie's eyes, handed it across to her.

"I was clutching it tightly in my right hand when they found us on the sands of that little bay near Uisken on Mull, and it wasn't until I was home and in bed that Mummy could persuade me to relax and open my hand. I suppose it was because Calum told me to keep it no matter what happened, until I was safely back in the cottage again."

"The beadbonny ash," Bridie murmured, fingering the twig with its now brittle leaves, its wrinkled orange-red berries. Whether it came from a mountain ash savaged by wild swine centuries ago in Dalriada, or from the rowan which grew at the front door of the cottage on Mull, Bridie did not know. It had protected them from people and from creatures who would have harmed them, and that was all that mattered. "The beadbonny ash," she repeated softly.

"Keep it," Sheena said, closing Bridie's fingers round it.

"In case we need it again?" Bridie asked gravely.

"Oh, no. Just because it is—the beadbonny ash." And they smiled at each other; at that moment neither was superstitious, but all the same. . . .

"You know," Kenneth said, "It was all so terribly exciting at the time, and we all had to make such important decisions, that you'd think it would have had some kind of an effect on us. But it hasn't. At least not on me. I feel exactly the same as I did before, except for one thing. I'm jolly glad I live now. No 'good old days' for me—ever."

"I suppose," Sheena said thoughtfully, "that I ought to assert myself a bit more. But I don't expect I shall."

"You don't need to," Bridie assured her. "You'll always get your own way in the end, just by being you." But there was no doubt of the effect on her of her dream of Dalriada. She had worked right through her unhappiness and had learned—no!—was still learning how to come to terms with other people and, what was far more difficult, with herself.

"I nearly forgot," Kenneth said suddenly. "There's a letter for you, Bridie. From John. At least it's his rotten handwriting. It's funny, because he always phones and never writes. If you ask me. . . ."

"We didn't," Sheena said firmly.

"O.K. I was only going to say he doesn't like them pink or scented. And neither do I."

"I'll remember when I write to you," Bridie promised. A letter from John—who never wrote. Whatever was in it, she'd reply, of course. Ordinary politeness demanded that. Would he write a second time? And a third? She was almost sure that he liked her quite a lot, but it would be at least a year before they'd see each other again. In twelve months they'd both meet lots of people . . . change . . . at least she'd change, and she hoped it'd be for the better. But however much she changed, there was one thing she was certain of: there'd never be anyone like

John. Never.

Suddenly she jumped and cried out in alarm. Taken by surprise at the sudden blaze of light in which they found themselves, the other two gasped and then laughed to find themselves illuminated along with McCaig's Tower—the folly which some people found ridiculous, but which Bridie loved because her friends, the MacDonalds, admired it.

"Come on, chaps," Kenneth shouted, running off into the darkness. "I'm hungry and I think it's Finnan haddies for tea. Or it may be Arbroath smokies."

"Does it matter?" Bridie asked, as she and Sheena followed more slowly. "I like them both. I think I could go on eating them for ever."

"And they all lived happily ever after, and had haddocks and kippers for tea every day," Sheena said, and they all burst out laughing because there was room in life for such simple, ridiculous things.

As she stopped laughing, Bridie halted a moment to look down again on the lights streaming from hotels and shops and houses, dipping on the masts of moored craft which rose and fell with the tide, flashing and winking from distant lighthouses—and she knew now she could return to London and live there contentedly with her mother and stepfather.

She would come back to Scotland again of course, accept the Mac-Donalds' invitation to stay here with them in Oban, go back with them to Mull and learn to love the Western Highlands and the Hebridean islands as they did.

But Barra she would visit alone, because somewhere on that island there might be people who would welcome and talk to her because they were related to her, and there would surely be others who could recall tales told about Bridie O'Neill; and when at last she was able to visualize her great-great-grandmother as a real person, then, perhaps, she would be able to complete that understanding of herself begun in her dream of—or return to—Dalriada.